I0636704

HAPPILY NEVER AFTER

A RANDALL & CARVER MYSTERY

RANDALL & CARVER MYSTERIES
BOOK TWO

BLAIR HOWARD

Copyright © 2024 Happily Never After by Blair Howard
All rights reserved.

Cleveland, TN, United States of America
ISBN Print: 979-8-9908529-3-8
Library of Congress Control Number: 2024922780

No part of this publication may be reproduced, stored in a retrieval system, or transmitted in any form, or by any means, electronic, mechanical, photocopying, recording, or otherwise, without the express written permission of the publisher except for the use of brief quotations in a book review.

Disclaimer: Happily Never After is a work of fiction. The persons and events depicted in this novel are the creation of the author's imagination; no resemblance to actual persons or events is intended.

Product names, businesses, brands, and other trademarks referred to within this book are the property of the respective trademark holders and are used fictitiously. Unless otherwise specified, no association between the author and any trademark holder is expressed or implied. Nor does the use of such trademarks indicate an endorsement of the products, trademarks, or trademark holders unless so stated. Use of a term in this book should not be regarded as affecting the validity of any trademark, registered trademark, or service mark.

www.blairhowardbooks.com

Contact: blairhoward@blairhowardbooks.com

For my beautiful Daughter Mallory

PROLOGUE

WHO KILLED FRANNY MCNEER?

Extract from Thomas Drews' podcast dated March 15, 2022: *Who Killed Franny McNeer?*

...assuming Luthor McNeer didn't kill his wife as he has always claimed, we must substitute "It" for "He" or "She" when referencing the killer. And I must warn you, I take a little literary license in my narrative.

At almost midnight on the evening of Friday, July 8, 2016, the killer crept into the McNeer bedroom. Franny McNeer was asleep, alone, in the marital bed, snoring softly, perhaps even dreaming.

The killer stood for a moment in the light of the full moon, staring down at her, knife in hand, then stepped around the bed, took a deep breath, raised the knife and plunged it through the covers into the sleeping woman's breast, and then withdrew it and plunged it again and again and again into

Franny's body, each blow more savage than the one before until the killer, exhausted by its efforts, stepped away, blood dripping from the knife blade. Franny McNeer died quickly. Nineteen of the forty-three stab wounds would have been fatal; this according to Dr. Sheddon, the Hamilton County Chief Medical Examiner. An act of rage, he called it, and rage it must have been for her assailant to stab her so many times.

We know from the bloody footprints that, eventually, the killer took a step back, and the knife, slippery with blood, slid from its fingers and fell to the floor. The killer then turned away and walked quickly and silently from the room, leaving a trail of bloody footprints on the carpet. Franny McNeer, her eyes wide, stared sightlessly up at the ceiling.

Two days later, Luthor McNeer, Franny's husband, was arrested and charged with her murder. It was Luthor who discovered his wife's body. He claimed to have been asleep downstairs on the couch in the living room when something disturbed him and he went upstairs and found her in their blood-soaked bed. He immediately went to her and held her in his arms, but it was too late.

Luthor, now with blood on his clothes and his shoes, called the emergency services and was found standing beside the bed. Of course, he claimed he had nothing to do with her death, but his was the only DNA found at the scene, and there were no signs of an intruder, even though Luthor swore all the doors and windows were locked. The knife handle, slick with the victim's blood, was devoid of fingerprints.

Was Luthor McNeer asleep on the couch as he claims? Was it an intruder that brutally murdered Franny McNeer? In either case, the police didn't think so, and Luthor had no explanation as to why he'd slept through the horrific murder. He denied he was drunk, and blood analysis proved it to be true. Nor were there drugs in his system. So how could he have slept through it all? Luthor himself has no explanation.

Luthor was tried for his wife's murder and was found guilty and sentenced to twenty-five years to life imprisonment. He always claimed he was innocent. But if it wasn't him… who did kill Franny McNeer, and why?

1

MONDAY, NOVEMBER 18, 2024

8am

"Annie, will you please get yourself in here?" Mallory shouted.

The dog stopped its sniffing, turned and gave her a look of disdain. Rarely did Mallory raise her voice to the Border Collie, but it was eight-thirty on a Monday morning in November. It was cold and drizzling with rain outside, and Mallory was not looking forward to the week ahead. Work of late had been, well, boring. A long-running financial investigation—one of Tucker's many fortes—three nasty divorce cases and a missing person case, only the person wasn't missing at all. She'd simply taken an unannounced leave of absence and had checked herself into a Benedictine convent for a month to "Find my inner self." Even so, it had taken all of Tucker's many skills to track her down, whereupon she'd told him in no uncertain terms to F off and leave her alone with the nuns.

Mallory, a one-time-bartender with a penchant for organization and true crime podcasts, had joined Tucker Randall's one-man organization almost a year earlier after he solved the disappearance of her beloved niece, Julie, with unwavering help from Mallory. Unfortunately, though, the investigation ended in tragedy when it was discovered that Julie had been murdered by Dr. John Williams, a local family GP.

Jennifer Romero, Mallory's older sister and Julie's mother, had hired Tucker, an ex-FBI special agent and something of a loner, to find her missing daughter. Mallory had, much to Tucker's chagrin, insisted on sticking her nose in. At first, he wanted nothing to do with Mallory or her in-depth research. But, as the case wore on, and Tucker, unused to the great outdoors, began to flounder and soon realized that Mallory was much more than the ditsy bartender he'd thought her to be. Thus was born an unusual alliance between the two, and, when the case was brought to its tragic conclusion, he offered her a job as a kind of junior partner. Little did he know what he was letting himself in for.

"Annie," Mallory snapped at the dog, her eyes narrowed, "if you don't come inside right now..." She let the threat dangle unfinished. Annie, smarter even than the average Border Collie, got the message and slunk past her into the office and over to her bed, where she sat down and stared defiantly at her mistress.

"I swear you get worse by the day," she muttered, then went to the door that opened into Randall's home, opened it and yelled, "TUCKER, are you coming, or what?" Then she turned away and went to her desk and sat down.

"Geez, what is wrong with you?" Tucker said as he walked

through the door, his jacket over his arm. "You have a rough weekend or something?"

"No," she replied, "but we need to talk. We're hemorrhaging money, and these stupid divorce cases aren't helping. We need something more… meaty. Something we can get our teeth into. Something with a decent paycheck."

"Something *I* can get my teeth into, you mean," he replied with a grin.

"Oh, dear Lord," she said, rolling her eyes. "I'm doing all the work as it is and…" She paused, gave him a grossly exaggerated frown, and then continued. "Speaking of that. Isn't it time you gave me a raise?"

He made a face, shook his head and said, "And what would I pay you with? You just said we're… How did you put it? Oh, yes, hemorrhaging money." He grinned at her triumphantly.

She smiled sweetly at him and said, "How about from that rainy-day account you failed to tell me about?"

"But it's not raining—"

"Oh, yes, it is," she said. "Go outside and look."

"That's not what I meant, and you know it," he said, then sat down in the guest chair in front of his desk. "But you're right. We do need something to pump a little life into things, even if it means we have to travel. There's this thing we've been dodging in Shreveport; well, you've been dodging it."

"Tucker, there has to be plenty to do around here without us having to go gallivanting off into the bayous. Don't you think?"

"I'd hardly call Shreveport bayou country," he retorted. "And, if there's plenty to do around here, as you say, why aren't we getting any of it?"

"Because you're old-fashioned and won't let me do some marketing."

"Marketing? What do you know about marketing?"

"I know if people don't know you're here, they can't hire you," she said.

"So what do you suggest?" he asked, crossing his legs and folding his arms.

"I suggest we hire a marketing company to get our name out there. I've been doing some research... and don't look at me like that. Stop grinning at me, too. You look like... You look silly. Anyway, I found two companies I think might do a good job. What do you think?"

"I think..." he said and paused, smiling at her, "that if I don't let you do as you please, you'll make my life hell. So go ahead and look into it. But do *not* spend any money without checking with me first. Understood?"

"Understood," she replied. "Now, how about that raise?"

"Forget it," he said, uncrossing his legs and rising to his feet when the phone rang.

"Randall and Carver," Mallory said. "How can I help you?"

"Mallory, is that you?"

Mallory frowned. "Vinnie?"

2

"It's Vinnie McNeer," she mouthed with her hand over the phone.

"Hey, Mal. How you doin'?"

"Vinnie..." Mallory hesitated, then said, "I'm doing fine. To what do I owe this honor?"

"You're doin' okay, then, you and that Randall fella?"

"I am, but... Vinnie, I haven't heard from you in almost a year, and we didn't part on the best of terms—"

"Forget about all that," Vinnie interrupted her. "I need to talk to you. Can you come on over?"

"What d'you want, Vinnie?"

"Not on the phone, Mal. I just need... Just come on over, will you? I'll buy you a beer, or whatever." And with that, he hung up, leaving Mallory staring at the phone.

She put the phone back onto its cradle. "He wants to talk," she said, still frowning.

"What about? Did he say?"

Mallory shook her head. "No. He just said he needed to talk and that he'd buy me a beer, and then he hung up. What d'you think? Do you think he's finally gotten around to suing me for the damage I did to his liquor stock?"

She was referring to the day she quit her job at The Saloon and cleared the high-end liquor shelf as she walked out, smashing hundreds of dollars' worth of expensive bottles of scotch, brandy, bourbon, gin and tequila. Vinnie had promised to make her pay for it all but had never followed up... *Until now?* she wondered.

Mallory had worked for Vinnie as his principal bartender for more than ten years until that day when he crossed the line and accused her of having sex with Tucker, at which point she'd lost it.

Tucker shook his head and said, "Nah! If he said he wants to talk to you, that's probably what he wants. He wouldn't offer free beer if he was planning a lawsuit. I think you should go. You want me to go with you?"

"I dunno, Tucker. What if he... Perhaps he..." She shrugged. "I dunno. It's been almost a year. D'you think...? Oh, hell. Let's do it. What have I got to lose except a bunch of money? Yeah, come with me."

She grinned at him, then said, "You should have seen it, Tucker. He almost blew a gasket. The place was in an uproar. I gotta tell you. It was hilarious."

"But possibly costly," Tucker replied, clearly not amused.

"Killjoy," she said as she gathered up her phone and bag.

———

The Saloon hadn't changed. It was like stepping back in time to a less-than-pleasant era.

Vinnie McNeer was behind the bar wiping a glass, not something Mallory had seen him do more than a couple of times in the ten years she'd worked for him. And he looked nervous, which, to Mallory, seemed out of character. Vinnie, she knew, was the kind of guy who didn't give a damn about anyone or anything except money. And she wondered if she'd been right about an impending lawsuit after all.

"Hey, Mal, Tucker," Vinnie said, putting the glass down. "Good to see you both. Thanks for comin'. What can I get ya? It's on me, okay?" He squinted at them through his steel-framed glasses.

"Nothing for me," Mallory replied. "What is it you want, Vinnie?"

"I'm good," Tucker said before Vinnie could answer.

Vinnie McNeer was a big man. Not tall—about five-ten—but heavy. Some would describe him as stocky. He was broad-shouldered, barrel-chested with an enormous beer belly. He was also bald as a coot. Mallory had never been able to figure out how old he was. She'd asked him once, but he'd just smiled at her and ignored the question.

"Let's sit down," he said as he threw his cloth onto the counter at the back of the bar, then lifted the trap and came out into the room. "Over there," he said. "Where it's quiet."

Over there was a booth in the far corner of the room.

"Geez, Vinnie," Mallory said as they sat down. She and Tucker on one side of the table, and Vinnie facing them on the other. "If you're planning on suing me over the liquor thing, I'm sorry. I lost it and, if you'll give me a bill, I'll pay—"

"Nah!" he said, interrupting her. "That was over and done with a long time ago, and I don't blame you, anyway. I was outta line, what I said, and I should be the one to apologize. I'm sorry, Mal, and I hope you can forgive me."

"Of… course," she replied, frowning. "So, if it's not the liquor, why are we here?"

He squinted down at his fingernails, then looked up at her and said, "Mal, you worked for me for a long time. You know just about everything there is to know about me and my business, but I don't think I ever told you I have a younger brother."

He was right. Mallory had just turned twenty-one when she went to work at The Saloon. Back then, she was a skinny, five-eight natural blonde: a perky, extroverted, smart, witty, observant, talkative individual. Since then, she matured into something quite different; still five-eight. Still blonde. Still perky, extroverted, and talkative, but now, eleven years on, she was also obsessively organized, analytical, thoughtful, and empathetic. And she'd made herself almost indispensable to Tucker's business, something she knew he'd never admit.

Tucker, thirty-five, six-one with black hair and blue eyes, was a good-looking man, well-built, athletic, who worked out for thirty minutes or so almost every day, though he wasn't overly buff. He was a lone wolf kind of PI with a master's degree in criminology and a reputation for solving crime, preferring to work on his own and be left alone in the process. Mallory liked to think she was the bridge between him and the rest of the world.

He was a skeptic with a dry sense of humor. He told Mallory he'd been single most of his life, with just a couple of memorable girlfriends, but that was his fault. She saw that his dedication to his work left little time for a social life, even though he was handsome enough to date any pretty much any woman he wanted.

When she first met Tucker, she got the sense that he couldn't stand her. He found her overtly voluble and annoying. But Mallory had a way of growing on him and, by the time the puzzle of her missing niece had been solved, they'd become something of a team, though Tucker would never admit it at the time.

"He lived out in Polk County, in Greasy Creek," Vinnie continued. "His wife was a sweet girl. We all loved her…" He trailed off, obviously lost in thought.

Mallory paled at the sound of the name Greasy Creek. It held so many memories for her, all of them bad, but she said nothing, and Vinnie continued, "He never came in here…" Vinnie paused for a second, then continued. "Well, he did, but that was before your time. Me and him, we never really got along though and—"

"Vinnie," she said, interrupting him, a concerned expression on her face. "No, you never told me about him. What's happened? Is he dead?"

Vinnie held up his hand and smiled. It was a weary smile, and she could tell something was seriously wrong.

"There you go," he said. "That's the Mal Carver I knew, always jumping to conclusions before she's even heard me out. Let me tell you and then you'll know, okay? But first, I need to show you something."

He reached into his jacket pocket, pulled out a folded newspaper clipping, unfolded it, laid it out on the table and smoothed out the folds, then turned it around so they could see it.

Polk County Man Arrested for Brutal Slaying.

Luthor McNeer was arrested today for the murder of his wife, Franny McNeer. He claims he is innocent despite the mountain of evidence… and the article went on to describe the events of the night of July 8, 2016, in graphic detail.

Mallory read every word, and then she read it again. Then she looked up at him and said, "Vinnie, that's terrible. I don't know what to say."

"He didn't do it, Mal," he replied.

Of course he didn't, she thought cynically. *They never do!*

"That's what they all say," Tucker said. "Whoa, hold on." He held up his hand when he saw Vinnie was about to explode, then said, "Why don't you tell us why we're here, Vinnie?"

"I want you to find who really killed Franny," he said. "Look, Luthor is many things, but he ain't no killer, and he loved her. I know my brother, and I know he didn't do it. That no-good sheriff and his idiot son hung it on him and then quit lookin'. That's Polk County justice for ya. Look, I've been savin' me money for almost eight years. I can pay ya."

He reached into the inner pocket of the worn black leather jacket, pulled out a fat brown envelope, and dropped it on the table in front of Tucker. Mallory reached out, grabbed it, and opened it. It was stuffed full of hundred-dollar bills.

"There's ten thousand there," Vinnie said, "and I have more if you need it."

"Give it back, Mallory," Tucker said, staring at Vinnie, his eyes narrowed.

"Er... No!" Mallory replied.

"I said, give it back to him," Tucker snapped and reached for the envelope. But Mallory leaned away, holding the envelope above her head.

"Not until you hear him out," she said. "This could be just what we're looking for. I know the Cundiffs. You don't. And I believe him when he said they quit looking. That's just like them. Kal Cundiff is a lazy, good-for-nothing dumbass. The word 'work' is an anathema to him."

"It's a whata?" Vinnie said, screwing up his face as if in pain.

"It means he doesn't like work," Mallory explained.

"Oh that. Yeah, you're right about that," Vinnie said, grinning at her. "He's kinda sweet on you, though. Ain't he, Mal?"

"He's a pain in the ass," she replied.

"Look," Vinnie said. "You worked for me for almost ten years. And I always treated you good, didn't I? I mean... He didn't do it. You know?"

Mallory looked at Tucker. His face was a blank slate. She could tell he wasn't buying it.

"Why don't you tell us about it, Vinnie?" she said gently.

Vinnie nodded and said, "So... You see, someone broke into their house, and, well, it was late. I mean, like real late. Midnight. Franny was asleep in bed. Luthor had fell asleep on the couch downstairs... in the living room. And someone got in and stabbed Franny forty-three times. Luthor never heard a thing. He slept right through it. Sometime after midnight, he goes up to bed and he finds her. He tries to resusck... Re..."

"Resuscitate," Mallory said.

"Yeah, that," he said, nodding, "but she's dead, see? So, he calls 911, and that's it. He has blood on his clothes and his shoes and... And Luthor, well, he always was a heavy sleeper. Sleep through a bomb blast, he would." He shook his head at the memory, then continued. "They arrested him two days later. They didn't believe his story, and they didn't look no further. Damn Cundiffs."

Mallory, seeing how upset he was, reached out across the table, took his hand in hers and squeezed it.

Tucker stared at Vinnie for a moment, then said, "I don't believe it either. How could someone sleep through something like that?"

"According to the medical examiner, it was probably the first stab what killed her, so she didn't scream," Vinnie said.

"Why now, Vinnie?" Mallory asked.

"You think I have the kind o' money lyin' around it takes to hire a good investigator, girl? Hell no. I had to save it. That there…" He nodded at the envelope still in Mallory's hand. "… represents the better part of my life savings. You'll do it for me, won't you, Mal? I mean, he swears he didn't do it."

"What about appeals?" Tucker asked.

"Nah!" Vinnie replied with a grimace. "He basically shut down when he went inside. Never did appeal. I think he's accepted the fact he ain't never gonna get out. He misses Franny terrible like. He never sez much about it, but I can tell."

"So, if he didn't kill his wife, who does he think did?" Tucker asked.

"He won't talk about it," Vinnie replied. "All he'll say is he doesn't know and that it wasn't him. I don't know either. Franny was a nice kid, you know? Sweet, lovin', pretty… Damn!"

"I'm going to have to think about it, Vinnie," Tucker said. "Ouch! That hurt, Mallory. What the hell?"

"There's nothing to think about," she snapped. "Vinnie needs our help. It's what we do. And we need something to get our teeth into. Something that isn't so damn boring."

"*I said…* we'd think about it," he said. "And that's what we'll do. Look, we can't just go off half-cocked. We know nothing about the case. We need to do some research. Figure some things out. And, if we decide to take it on, we'll come up with a strategy. Now, give the man his money back."

Reluctantly, she did as he asked and handed the envelope back to Vinnie.

Tucker leaned forward, placed his hands together on the table, looked Vinnie in the eye and said, "We'll be in touch." He looked at Mallory, then back at Vinnie and continued,

"And if we do decide to take it on, you can pay us then. For now... Well, we'll see. Let's go, Mallory."

"Vinnie—" Mallory began, but he cut her off.

"It's okay, Mal. I get it. Me an' Luthor, we're just a couple of low-lives, always have been, and—"

"No, you're not," she snapped. "Like Tucker said. We'll be in touch. *I'll* be in touch. So you just hang in there, okay?"

Vinnie nodded despondently, then shook his head, stuffed the envelope in his jacket pocket, stood up, turned away, and walked slowly back to the bar.

"Tucker," she snapped. "Sometimes I could... I just don't get you."

"I know," he said, smiling.

3

They were both quiet on the ride back to the office, though Tucker kept glancing at Mallory, who remained stoically quiet, which was, to say the least, a little unusual and more than a little unnerving.

She spent most of the ride on her phone researching the Luthor McNeer case, and though Vinnie had made it clear the crime had been committed in Polk County, she was a little disturbed to see it had happened in Greasy Creek, a place that held so many sad memories.

"Okay," Tucker said, finally. "What have I done?"

"You refused to take Vinnie's money," she said without looking up from her phone.

"No, I didn't. I said we'd look into it and get back to him."

"But you don't want to take the case, do you?" she asked, still scrolling through the pages.

"No. I can't say I do," he replied.

"Why not?"

"For one, I don't like cold cases. They're time-consuming

and expensive, and they rarely end satisfactorily. Two, we'll be dealing with the Cundiffs again. Geez, Mallory, I don't want us to get embroiled in a repetition of your sister's case. That wouldn't be good for you. And three, I hate that frickin' forest."

She looked up at him and smiled. "I'll make an outdoorsman of you yet. But look, it wouldn't require any travel, and I hate travel." She paused for a moment, then said, "You know, it was a big case in its day. Eight years ago, I was working for Vinnie. How come I've heard nothing about it? Why did he never mention it? I don't get it."

"Vinnie's a strange cat," Tucker replied. "He's a loner. No friends that I've ever seen. Have you?"

She shook her head.

Tucker thought for a minute, then said, "There's a lot more crime that happens under the radar than on it, especially when it's a domestic violence case. I don't like it, Mallory. I don't think we should take it. Look, I had a text from a family in Tulsa. Their daughter—"

"You can forget that," she snapped, interrupting him. "I'm not going to spend Christmas in Oklahoma away from my home and family where I don't know a soul or the area. Not when we have a perfectly good case with good money right here at home, and cash, too. So you can forget it. Either that, or you can go on your own, and I'll work Vinnie's case by myself."

"You?" He laughed. "You'll work it? D'you really think you could?"

"Look, Tucker. I may not be a smarty-pants FBI agent, but I know the fundamentals of how to conduct an investigation. I've been studying ever since you hired me. So yes, I think I could."

"You really are something, Mallory," he replied, shaking his head as he pulled into the driveway. "But you know what? I wouldn't be surprised if you could."

"So, no Oklahoma, then?"

"No. No Oklahoma," he replied, rolling his eyes.

"And we'll take Vinnie's case?"

"I didn't say that. I said we'll look into it, and that's what we'll do," he said as he slid the key into the lock and turned it.

"And how d'you propose we go about that?" she asked as he stood aside for her to enter.

When he didn't reply after a second, she continued, "And I don't know what you're so hopped up about," she said as she went to start the coffee. "It's a cold case, yes, but it's a murder case, and we both like those."

"We *like* murder cases?" he asked. "Do you have any idea how that sounds?"

"Oh, come on, Tucker. You know what I mean. So, I'll ask you again. Where do we begin?"

"I think—" he began.

"You know what I think?" she said, cutting him off. "I think we should go talk to Luthor McNeer and see what he has to say. After all, there's nothing to say that Vinnie isn't simply in denial. And if Luthor isn't trying to get out of prison, maybe it's because he's actually guilty… And, if he is, he might even admit it. Especially if we tell him how much money Vinnie is willing to spend. What do *you* think?"

"I think I'll just shut my mouth and let you do all the thinking," he replied dryly. "I was just about to suggest we go talk to him when you so rudely interrupted me."

"Oh, you were? Sorry. You want me to make an appointment, then?"

"Might as well," he replied. "It seems I have little to say about how we run things around here anymore."

She grinned at him. "You really are a big old softy at heart, aren't you, Tucker?"

"You think?" he said. "Just you wait."

She spent the next fifteen minutes on her phone, working her way through the prison bureaucracy and making an appointment for them both to visit Luthor at ten-thirty on Wednesday morning local time.

"Ten-thirty on Wednesday," she said. "That work for you?"

"I guess it will have to if you've already made the appointment. See what I mean when I say I have little to do with how we run things around here?"

"Now that's just not true, Tucker. I trust and I... respect you. So, we're good then?"

"Yes, we're good," he replied with a sigh.

"Good. Now, I've found something interesting. You want to hear it?"

"Do I have to?" he asked wearily.

"You don't, but you should," she replied. "It's one of Thomas Drews' podcasts dated March 15, 2022, and titled *Who Killed Franny McNeer?*"

"Really?" he replied, suddenly interested. "Well, okay then. Let's hear it."

The podcast lasted forty-four minutes, and when it was finished, Tucker leaned back in his chair, linked his hands together behind his neck and stared at the painting of Confederate General Nathan Bedford Forrest on the wall behind her.

She waited as long as she could, about thirty seconds, then said, "Well, what do you think?"

"I think..." he said, then paused, still staring at the painting.

"Oh my God, Tucker. You are so annoying. Are you going to tell me what you think, or not?"

He unclasped his hands from behind his neck, leaned forward, and said, "I think the podcast was interesting. Maybe we should talk to this Drews guy. He seems to know what he's doing. He's local, isn't he?"

"Yes. He's quite famous. He has more than a million followers and some pretty powerful friends in law enforcement. He's from here, local—"

"Okay. I get it," Tucker said, cutting her off. "See if you can set something up. In the meantime, we need a copy of the police file. You can handle that too, seeing as you're friendly with that A-hole of a sheriff." He grinned at her. She stuck out her tongue at him. Then made the call.

"Sheriff Cundiff," she began. "This is Mallory Carver. We're investigating the McNeer case— No— Not at all— What? No, of course not— I'm— Of course. Why not? So, you're refusing to cooperate! I wonder what the press will make of that. Huh? Oh, but I would. No, I don't care. Thank you. When can I come and pick it up? Sounds good. I'll see you in an hour, then." She hung up and looked at Tucker.

"That went well," he said.

"He didn't want to give it to me," she replied, rising to her feet.

"So I gathered," he said, dryly.

"Can I leave Annie here with you?"

"You left her here on her own this morning, so I don't see why not. Don't be long. I'm hungry. And stay clear of that Cundiff kid. He's bad news."

"Hah, jealous, are we?"

He looked up at her grinning and said, "As if!"

_____

Mallory told Annie to be a good girl and then went out to her car. She pushed the starter button, checked the gas, saw she had three-fourths of a tank, then she backed out of the driveway and headed west toward I-75. From there, she headed north to Exit 20 and from there to Highway 64 and Benton, Tennessee.

The Polk County Justice Center was just off Highway 314 on Industrial Access Circle, about a forty-five-minute drive from Tucker's home office. She made it in forty minutes and arrived in the parking lot at eleven-fifteen to find Deputy Kal Cundiff lounging out front, smoking a cigarette.

"Mal," he said, stepping forward as she slid out of her CRV, "Dad... I mean, the sheriff said you were coming. What's this I hear about you guys investigating the McNeer case? I can't see why you would. It was a slam dunk, and he got life. Case closed."

"How've you been, Kal?" she asked.

"Me? I'm good. You?"

"Yes, I'm fine. You want to take me to the sheriff?"

"Yeah, 'course, but you didn't answer my question. Why are you working that old chestnut? Waste of time, if you ask me?"

"I'm not asking you, Kal. Now, will you take me to your dad, or shall I go find him by myself?"

"Okay," he said, frowning. "But I—"

"*Kal?*" she snapped, interrupting him.

"Okay, okay. Keep your hair on. It's this way. Follow me."

Sheriff Kevin Cundiff, an older man in his early sixties, tall with white hair, a heavy gut and a military bearing, was seated at his desk. Just behind him and to his right, his chief deputy, Ryan Wilks, was standing at parade rest: shoulders back, chest out, hands clasped behind his back.

Cundiff rose and extended his hand across his desk to Mallory.

"It's good to see you again, Miss Carver... It is still miss, I take it?"

"If you're asking if I'm married, Sheriff, the answer is no, but it's nice to see you too."

"Please, sit down," Cundiff said, then looked at Kal and said, "That's all, Deputy. You may leave now."

Kal backed out of the door, looking decidedly disappointed.

"You know Chief Deputy Wilks?" Cundiff asked.

"No. I'm sorry, I don't. It's nice to meet you, Chief."

Wilks nodded but remained silent.

"So, talk to me, Mal," Cundiff said. "What's going on? Why are you investigating the McNeer case?"

She stared at him for a moment, wondering what to say and how to say it without upsetting him. She decided the best approach was to tell him the truth.

"We're not actually investigating it... yet. Vinnie, Luthor McNeer's brother and... Well, I worked for Vinnie for nearly ten years. Anyway, he asked us to look into it, so we're in the process of deciding whether or not to take the case. Tucker Randall, my boss... You remember him, right? He doesn't want to take the case, but I think we should. Maybe Luthor's innocent. Maybe he isn't. Either way, Vinnie would like to know. He'd like either closure for himself or his brother set free. Me, I think maybe the original investi… Well, you get the idea, I'm sure. So, do you have the file for me? If so, I'd like to be on my way… What?"

"Geez, girl," Cundiff said, shaking his head. "You haven't changed a bit, have you? You can still talk the hind leg off a donkey." He was smiling when he said it, and Mallory felt a little embarrassed that he'd said it in front of his chief deputy, but she just tilted her head a little to the right, opened her eyes wide, smiled, and stared at him.

"Why don't you finish what you were going to say?" Cundiff asked, leaning back in his chair.

"Oh, I don't think that's necessary," Mallory replied. "Now, can I have the file or not?"

"You were going to say you thought the original investigation was botched, weren't you?" he said quietly, *and a little menacingly*, she thought.

She simply shrugged and continued to stare at him.

"Why would you think that?" he asked.

"Was it botched?" she asked, unsure of how to handle the increasingly difficult conversation.

"Of course not," he replied. "We exercised proper due diligence, analyzed the evidence and the facts, and came to the only logical conclusion that Luthor McNeer stabbed his wife to death. There were no other suspects, and yes, we looked. Now, take the file…" He leaned forward, picked up a thick manila file folder, and tossed it across the desk. "But listen to me carefully, Mal. Think hard before you decide to take this on, because if you do, and if you cause me any more trouble, like you did last year, I'll sue you and your boss. I'll bankrupt you both. I'll own your homes. Now get out of here before I change my mind."

Mallory took a deep breath, nodded, then stood up, picked

up the file and, without saying a word, turned and walked quickly out of his office and out into the parking lot.

Well, that went well, she thought as she started the car. *I wonder what his problem is? Can't be little old me. Maybe he's worried we might find something.*

4

"So," Mallory said, "Do we talk to Thomas Drews or not?"

"Eh, I'm not a fan of podcasters and wannabe amateur detectives."

"Wow, did you ever get that wrong?" she replied. "Drews is... well, he was, until he retired a few years ago, a highly decorated and respected detective lieutenant with the Miami PD. I think he probably knows what he's talking about, don't you, Mr. FBI? So he's a podcaster now. So what? It's always good to get another perspective. You said that to me before, and I think—"

"Okay," Tucker said, interrupting her and throwing up his hands. "Talk to him, if you can. But how're you going to do that? These people don't give out their phone numbers to just anyone."

"I'm not just anyone," she replied with a disarming smile. "I already have his number."

"Oh yeah? How come?"

"He's a friend of Kate's."

"Kate? Who's Kate?"

"Kate Gazzara," Mallory replied. "She's a captain with the Chattanooga PD. She's a friend, kinda. I met her at the range. She's quite nice, for a cop. Anyway, she gave it to me."

"Oh, and why would she do that?"

"I asked her for it."

"Oh, come on, Mallory. Don't make me drag it out of you."

"Okay... Okay," she said. "As you know, I'm a big fan of true crime in all its forms, especially podcasts. I have several favorites. Devin Rudd is one, and Thomas Drews is another. I talk to Devin on his Facebook group, and I happened to find out through various channels... well, Kate, actually. She told me that Drews lives in Dalton and that she knows him. Me? I think she more than knows him; I think she's seeing him. It was ages ago; last March, I think. So I called her and told her that you and I were partners and that I needed to talk to him and... Well, I told her I was interested in his Weston case podcast, which I was, and that I had a question, so she gave me his number and... I called him." Mallory shrugged, tilted her head and smiled at him. Then she made a face.

"And how did that go?" Tucker asked skeptically.

Again, she shrugged, then said, "Not as well as I'd hoped. He was courteous, asked me how I had gotten his number— which I didn't tell him, of course—then he thanked me but said he didn't discuss his cases and he... hung up."

"And you think he'll talk to you after that faux pas?" Tucker asked, leaning back in his chair. "I sure as hell wouldn't."

"Probably not," Mallory replied, "but..." She lowered her chin and looked at him seductively through her eyelashes, pouted and said, "I was hoping you might call him, and I could listen in."

"Don't you do that—" he began, but she cut him off.

"Do what? Come on, Tucker. The guy's already done most of the footwork. What have we got to lose?"

"No!"

She actually stamped her foot, then folded her arms across her stomach and glowered at him.

"Why the hell not?" she snapped.

"Because…" and it was then he realized he didn't have a good answer.

"I get it," she said, the snark thick in her voice. "It's because you didn't think of it. Well, that's kind of petty, don't you think?"

"That's not what… Oh, what the hell. Have it your way. What's the number?"

She smiled while wiggling in her seat and gave him the number.

He glared at her for a moment, then picked up his phone and dialed the number. Drews answered on the second ring.

"This is Thomas."

"Good afternoon, Mr. Drews. This is Tucker Randall. I'm the managing partner at Randall and Carver Private Investigations in Chattanooga. I was wondering if you had time for a quick word?"

Drews was silent for a moment, then said, "Of course. What about?"

"We've been asked to look into the McNeer murder, and during our research, we came across your podcast…" He paused and glared at Mallory, who was signaling animatedly and mouthing "speaker."

"Hold on a minute, Mr. Drews, while I put you on speaker so my *secretary* can listen in. There, now, as I was saying—"

"What more can I tell you, Mr. Randall? I remember that

podcast. It was an in-depth and thorough narrative of my investigation. Listen to it. You'll find it's all there."

"I have, and you're right, Mr. Drews," Tucker replied. "You covered all the bases, but you didn't offer any opinions. Those are what I'm looking for. Your personal insights. Did he do it? Did Luthor McNeer murder his wife?"

Drews was again silent for a moment, then said, "Honestly, I'm not sure. There was no sign of a break-in. He claims he was asleep on the couch when it happened. They found him covered in blood. And there was blood on his shoes. There was only one set of bloody shoe prints, and they proved to be his. That's all circumstantial, of course. But here's the thing. As far as anyone can tell, McNeer didn't have a motive. The argument was that no one could have slept through that kind of carnage. There were, of course, no fingerprints on the knife, but it was slick with blood, and, as I said, the only shoe prints were his."

He paused for a moment, then continued, "My thought is that the killer would have removed his shoes, and if the first stab wound killed the wife, then McNeer could indeed have slept through it all. I examined the doors and windows, and it's true, there were no signs of a break-in, but the house was old and so were the windows. They have simple catches, so all it would have taken is a thin blade or strip of steel, such as a Slim Jim, to unlatch any of the ground-floor windows. So, in my opinion, yes, he could be innocent, but I also think it's unlikely. Now, if you don't mind, I have an appointment. Goodbye, and good luck, Mr. Tucker. If it goes your way, please call me. I'd like to update my podcast." And he hung up.

They looked at each other. Tucker shrugged and put his phone down. Mallory went back to her desk, sat down and then stared at him, but he said nothing.

"So?" she asked, finally.

"He told us nothing we didn't already know, except for the windows. I, myself, thought the killer could have taken off his shoes; I would have. Guilty or not, I think a good lawyer might have gotten him off."

"Okay," Mallory replied. "So, our next step is to talk to Luthor, then?"

He thought for a moment, then nodded and said, "Yes. You made the appointment for Wednesday. That's good. I need time to think and to study the file. Oh, and by the way, you do realize that Luthor is under no obligation to talk to us. So don't go getting all uppity if he refuses."

"As if I would," she said, frowning.

"Oh yes, you would. I know you only too well."

She ignored him for a moment, then said, "I made the appointment for ten-thirty."

"That's eleven-thirty our time," Tucker said. "It's a two-and-a-half-hour drive, depending on the traffic, so we need to start out at…" He looked at his watch. *Why did he do that? Mallory wondered. It's almost three in the afternoon today.* "… seven o'clock, to be sure of getting through the rush hour traffic on I-24. You'll need to be here at six-thirty."

She was about to tell him to pick her up but then realized he'd have to make the trip both ways through the traffic, so she nodded her agreement.

"You want to look this over with me?" he asked as he picked up the file and rose to his feet. He stepped around the desk and walked over to the table set against the wall next to a large whiteboard.

"Sure," she said and joined him at the table.

The file was, in fact, a copy of the murder book containing the crime scene photographs, the investigating officer's notes, witness statements, autopsy report, tox reports, forensics reports, and a somewhat lengthy but lacking in substantive detail, summation by Sheriff Kevin Cundiff.

Mallory picked up one of the photographs, looked at it, cringed, then set it down again. "Wow," she whispered, almost to herself. "She must have really pissed someone off." Then she picked up the photo of Luthor covered in blood. His eyes looked as if they were about to pop out of his head.

"He looks terrified," she whispered. "Or crazy."

"I'd go for crazy," Tucker said, glancing sideways at the photo. "I know what an FBI profiler would make of that, and it's not good."

"He's not crazy," Mallory said. "He's just frightened, poor man, and so would you be, too, if you'd just found your wife murdered like that. I've seen that look before. It's the same one Vinnie had when he was threatened by some bikers over a double charge on their tab. You have no feelings, Tucker."

"Very funny," Tucker replied, then thought for a moment before continuing. "Yeah, well, I've met a lot just like him, and that photo doesn't fill me with confidence," Tucker said thoughtfully as he read the ME's report. "It says here the wounds were all concentrated in the chest area, and that any one of nineteen would have been fatal, and that there were no defensive wounds on her hands or arms." He glanced at Mallory and said, "So, she must have been asleep." He was stating the obvious, but it was more that he was thinking out loud than making conversation. "Which, if Luthor is to be believed," he continued, "is why the attack didn't wake him... It's possible, I suppose."

Together, they continued to go through the file almost in silence until, at last, Mallory said, "I don't know what you think, but there's a lot of filler here and no real substance.

Sure, they conducted interviews, but it seems to me they were just going through the motions, covering their asses. They made up their minds from the moment they walked on site that Luthor was the killer. That's what I think. What do you think, Tucker?"

He took a deep breath, blew it out through his nose, then nodded slowly. "I'm inclined to agree with you, but I'm not sure I wouldn't have come to the same conclusion."

"But, from what I can tell," Mallory said, "they never even did a search to see if there were any other similar deaths. Surely, that would be standard procedure, wouldn't it? I mean, it's what I would have done and will do when we get back from Nashville."

Again, Tucker nodded slowly, but this time he didn't reply. Instead, he picked up Luthor McNeer's mugshot and stared at it for a moment, then closed his eyes, tilted his head back and stared sightlessly up at the ceiling. Mallory said nothing. She'd seen him do it before. It meant he was deep in thought.

He opened his eyes, looked at her and said, "We're not going to do anything, not even think about it, until we've talked to McNeer."

5

WEDNESDAY, NOVEMBER 2024

They made the drive to Nashville almost in silence, which, for Mallory, was something of a strain. She wanted to talk about the case, but Tucker was having none of it, preferring instead to keep an open mind.

It was almost ten-fifteen when they arrived at the prison, a dour, imposing collection of tan-colored buildings with arrow slits for windows. They worked their way through the security systems, handed over their weapons, phones and keys until, finally, they were escorted into a large, public room wherein there were some thirty steel tables with seats attached. Some of them were occupied by inmates and their visitors; most were unoccupied.

A guard escorted them to a table where they were told to sit down and that "the inmate" would arrive shortly.

"So," Mallory said, looking around. "This is nice." It was meant to be humorous but somehow fell flat. There was nothing nice about it.

Tucker looked at her, smiled and said, "There's no need to be nervous. I've interviewed cons in rooms like this many times, many of them much worse than Luthor McNeer. You get used to it... eventually."

"I'm not nervous," she said quickly, a bit too quickly, he thought.

"Oh yes, you are," he replied. "I can tell. Just take a deep breath and relax."

She glared at him, then softened and said, "Can you imagine being locked away like this for the rest of your life? I can't. It must be an awful way to live."

"No, I can't," he replied and looked around at the guards. "And you haven't even seen the cells," he continued, "the way they actually live. Not only are they locked up, but they also have to be on their guard every second. One wrong word to the wrong person and it's a beating, or even worse, a shiv in the belly. An inmate's is a dangerous life."

Mallory looked at him, not knowing what to say. It was a subject she'd never thought about, and what he said had shocked her.

It was some fifteen minutes later when the man Mallory recognized from the mugshot was escorted to the table and ordered to sit.

His escort—guard, Mallory supposed—stood by until he was seated, then looked at Tucker and said, "You have one hour. No touching. I'll be over there." Then he turned away and went to the seat under the window and sat down.

Luthor didn't look happy. In fact, Mallory thought he seemed annoyed, irritated, even. *He looks like a younger version of Vinnie.* Mallory thought, *only better looking.*

"I know who you are," he said, looking at Tucker, then at

Mallory, "and you. You used to work for Vinnie. I don't like visitors. What are you doing here?"

"If you know who we are, Luthor," Tucker said, "then you know we're private investigators and that we're here at the behest of your brother, Vinnie. He says you're innocent, that you didn't kill your wife, and that he wants us to find out who did."

At that, Luthor slowly shook his head and looked... sad. "Waste of time," he said. "Ain't no one gonna find out what happened that night. I don't even know myself. Tell Vinnie not to waste his money. What's he payin' you, anyway?"

"We haven't decided if we're going to take the case yet," Tucker said, avoiding the question. "That will depend on you."

"Yeah, well. Like I told ya, it'd be a waste of time and Vinnie's money, so why don't you just go away and leave me be?"

"Oh, come on, Luthor," Mallory said. "You can't mean that. Help us to help you. What have you got to lose?"

He looked at her, looked her up and down, and obviously liked what he saw. "I didn't do it," he said after a long moment. "That son of a bitch Kal Cundiff took one look at my wife, then at me, and made up his mind. The rest of the investigation was pure bullcrap. They questioned me, took my statement, then charged me. Took 'em all of two days. That sound like a proper investigation to you? Look, I know it sounds crazy, but I gotta tell ya. When I went upstairs and found her like that, it all seemed like a frickin' dream. Bizarre, huh?"

Mallory stared at him, not knowing what to think of him. *He doesn't seem like a killer to me*, she thought, *but what do I know? I've only ever met one, and he was nothing like this.*

"What do you mean, it felt like a dream?" Mallory asked.

He took a deep breath, shook his head, and said, "I dunno.

It was like... I remember sort of wakin' up. You know? Like you do, then goin' back to sleep. I was dreamin' I was at the mall, but it was deserted, no one there, not even in the shops, even though the lights were on. It was weird. Then I woke up again. The TV was on. Jimmy Kimmel. That's all I remember. I must have gone back to sleep again because when I woke up again, Nightline was on. So I got up and went to the bathroom, then up to bed. And that's when I saw it, her, my wife Franny, I mean. I thought I was still dreamin'. I swear I didn't do it. I never heard a thing... not a damn thing."

"Were you drunk, Luthor, when you went to sleep?" Mallory asked.

"No, ma'am, I was not."

"Drugs?" she asked, locking eyes with him.

He looked away, then at her again, shook his head and sighed, "A little weed, is all. And a Trazadone. The doc prescribed it for me. I have trouble going to sleep. That stuff knocks me out in minutes, but I usually wake up around two or three and go to the bathroom. It's not addictive, and it's not a controlled substance. It just helps you to go to sleep. I was takin' one every night back then. Don't get nothin' like that in here. Sleep's a damn nightmare all by itself here."

Hmm, that would account for him not hearing anything, Mallory thought.

"I tried to resuscitate her," he continued, "but she was already gone. That's how I got blood on me, and I must have stepped in it, too. I ran downstairs, grabbed my phone, and called 911. Shit, they took one look at me and cuffed me. I remember Kal sayin' somethin' to me. What it was, I can't remember, but I do remember the shit-eatin' grin he had on his face. They didn't believe a word I said, none of 'em. And that's it. That's all I remember. So now d'you get it?" he asked angrily. "It's over. Done with. Too frickin' late. The horse done run away. Tell Vinnie I 'preciate it, but he's to save his money. Now, are we done?"

Mallory stared at him, and the more she thought about it, the more she was sure he was telling the truth.

"Not quite," Tucker said. "I'd like to ask a few questions, if you don't mind?"

Luthor shrugged but didn't answer.

"I take it that's a yes," Tucker said, so let's begin with this: "if you didn't do it, who do you think did?".

Luthor's eyes lightened up at that, and he leaned forward, looked Tucker in the eye and said, "I've been thinking about that, a lot. And the only thing I can come up with is it must have been like… a serial killer or something."

Mallory looked at Tucker. He was clearly trying not to laugh.

"See, I think Franny was bein' stalked," Luthor said, obviously unaware of what Tucker must have been thinking. "She never said nothin'," he continued, "but she'd been on edge, uneasy, like, you know? For a couple o' weeks or so. I thought nothin' of it at the time, but now, well, yeah."

"And there's no one you can think of that might have had a grudge against her?" Tucker asked.

Luthor made a face, the corners of his mouth turned down, and said, "Not that I know of. She was a sweet, gentle woman. She didn't deserve to die like that, you know?"

Mallory could see his eyes were watering, and she was moved.

"Could she have been having an affair?" Tucker asked.

"Frickin' hell, no!" Luthor shouted and immediately looked over at the guard, who was already rising to his feet.

Tucker looked at him and nodded, and he sat down again.

"No!" Luthor insisted. "She wasn't like that. She never flirted with no one. Shit, we'd been together since we was kids, since tenth grade. She was… I loved her, and she loved me."

Tucker stared at him. Mallory could tell he wasn't buying the serial killer idea, but she had no idea of what else he might be thinking.

"Luthor," she said. "If you didn't kill your wife, somebody did, and it was up close and personal, and that means it was someone who knew her and, by the violent nature of the attack, that someone was very angry, in a terrible rage. Who could she have upset so much that they would kill her like that?"

"I told ya. I don't know. If she'd pissed someone off, she would've told me, and I would have sorted it out for her. That's how we was. We trusted each other."

"Well," Tucker said. "Thank you for your time, Luthor. We'll think about it and decide what to do—"

"Don't bother," Luthor said, interrupting him. "I told ya. I don't want Vinnie wastin' his money on a lost cause. You tell him thank you for me, and tell him a visit would be nice."

"Luthor," Mallory said. "Vinnie loves you. He believes you, and he's very worried about you."

"Yeah, well," Luthor said, "there's not much I can do about that now, is there?"

To her surprise, Tucker bit his lower lip, tsked, and then said, "Look, Luthor, if there's anything else we should know…" He trailed off when he saw the smirk on Luthor's lips.

"I'll tell you what you should know," he said, leaning forward, his eyes narrowed to mere slits. "You didn't believe me when I said it might have been a serial killer, did you?

Well, maybe you should look up the Tiffany Delgado case, is what you should do." Then he leaned back, grinning, turned to the guard and said, "We're done here. You can take me back now."

He stood up, still grinning, cocked his head to one side and opened his eyes wide and smiled, as if to say, *that's got ya thinking, ain't it?* Then he said the name again, "Tiffany Delgado."

They stayed seated and watched as the guard escorted Luthor across the room to the door, where he stopped, turned again to look at them, smiled at them, nodded, and then disappeared through the door.

"Wow," Mallory said. "That came right out of the blue. D'you think he knows something, Tucker?"

"I think," he said, "he's one wily SOB, but…"

"But what?" she asked.

He slowly shook his head and said, "I have absolutely no idea."

6

"Come on, Tucker. Tell me what you think." Mallory said as she closed the car door.

"I think…" he said, smiling, "I'm hungry. How about you?"

"I think you're a selfish, annoying pig," she responded. "No, seriously, what d'you think about the case?"

"Let's find somewhere to eat and then we can talk about it," he replied. "That sound good?"

It was then that Mallory realized she hadn't had breakfast. "Okay," she replied. "Sounds good to me."

Mallory searched nearby restaurants on her phone, but by then they were already heading south on I-24, and the nearest one she could find was the Hickory Falls Restaurant, a few miles south of La Vergne near Smyrna.

It was just after noon local time when they arrived, and the parking lot was packed.

"Oh dear," Mallory complained. "We'll be here for hours."

But they weren't. The service was fast, and the food was excellent. They both ordered burgers and fries, and while they waited, they discussed the case in general and Luthor McNeer in particular. At least, Mallory did. And all the while, Tucker sat quietly, listening to her and smiling stoically. Though when she finally stopped for a breath, he had to admit she'd made a good case.

"By the way, what did you do with Annie?" he asked. "It's not like you to leave her alone for this long."

"Oh, Annie, yes," she said, frowning. "Mrs. Salter, my neighbor, promised to look in on her. She'll be fine. She sleeps most of the day, anyway. Tucker, did you even hear a word I said?"

"I did," he replied.

"And?" she asked.

"And I think you make an excellent case..."

She smiled at him.

"But..." he said.

She frowned at him. "But what?"

"Look," he said, "I agree with almost everything you've said. Luthor may not have killed his wife... Whoa!" He held up his hand as he saw she was about to speak. "I said he *may* not have killed his wife, but I tend to believe him, or I did until he tossed out that serial killer theory. But what I was going to say was that we need to think it through before we commit to spending any more of Vinnie's money. Today alone is going to cost him, and ten thousand isn't going to go very far."

"What about Tiffany Delgado?" she asked.

"Ah, yes, Tiffany Delgado," he replied. "Now, methinks our erstwhile convict has done some research and found something. What it is and how it might be relevant we won't know until *you* have done *your* research, so we must set that aside until you have. Now, if you don't mind, let's eat our food and be on our way, agreed?"

"You really are a pain in the butt sometimes, Tucker

Randall, but," she looked down at her as yet untouched food, hoping he wouldn't hear her stomach growling, and said, "Yes. Agreed."

It was after five when they finally arrived back in Chattanooga. The traffic through the Split was still heavy, and by the time they arrived back at Tucker's home, they were both tired and irritable.

"Go home, Mallory," Tucker said as he exited the car. "I'll see you in the morning, bright and early."

Mallory was about to argue but thought better of it, admitting to herself that it was probably a good idea and said, "Right. Have a good night, Tucker."

As she drove home that evening, she couldn't keep her mind from wandering back to what Luthor had said about the Tiffany Delgado case.

"It's… I dunno," she muttered. "We don't even know where it happened." *But I can soon fix that*, she thought as she swung the CRV onto her driveway and cut the engine.

She unlocked the front door and stepped inside to be met by a near-hysterical Annie. The dog's tail was wagging her entire rear end.

She knelt down and hugged her and, in return, received a slathering face-licking that sent her reeling back onto her backside.

"Okay, okay. Stop it. Hahaha. Stop it. I get it. I'm pleased to see you, too." She pushed the dog away and scrambled to her feet. "I bet you're hungry," she said. "Let's go see if I can find you something to eat, but first, you have to go potty."

At that, Annie turned and ran to the back door. Mallory let her out and watched her run down the backyard to the perimeter fence. She stood for a moment and stared at the dark silhouette of the distant mountains in Polk County that held so many memories, most of them bad, most of them generated only a year ago when she lost her niece, Julie, to a murderous doctor.

She heaved a sigh and closed the door, finally ready to admit she was tired. She went to the kitchen, washed Annie's bowl, took some homemade dog food from the refrigerator, added a goodly portion to the bowl and nuked it for a minute in the microwave. Then she went to let Annie in and finally, she set the bowl down and watched the dog inhale it. *Wow,* she thought. *She really loves that stuff, and it's so good for her. Much better than the kibble.*

She sat down at the kitchen table, wondering what she was going to eat. Truth be told, she wasn't really hungry. The burgers and fries in Smyrna had been more than filling, so she decided on an icy-cold hard-boiled egg from the fridge and a glass of Pinot Noir, and then she took both to the living room and set them down, along with her phone, on the coffee table beside her laptop.

She glanced at the TV, then shook her head, heaved a sigh and sat down, ready to admit she was tired out, but she was also restless, fidgety. She took a bite of the egg, set it back down on the paper plate, took a sip of wine, and looked down at the laptop.

"Oh, geez, Annie. Now look what you made me do," she snapped as the dog jumped up on the couch beside her, jiggled her arm and made her spill her wine. *Damn it. I should have changed my clothes. Now look at my pants. That's going to stain and it will never come out!*

She jumped up, went to the kitchen, struggled out of the pants, muttering "vinegar, vinegar, vinegar," and then ran to the cupboard, grabbed a bottle of white vinegar and dowsed the stained section of cloth with it, then put it under the cold water tap and gently massaged it. Next, she sprayed it with OxyClean and gently massaged it some more, then washed it all out with warm water. *Best I can do*, she thought. *I'll leave them to soak overnight. Hopefully, that will do the trick. Now, jammies, then Tiffany Delgado.*

Five minutes later, she was back downstairs and back on the couch. She squinted, bared her teeth, sucked in a deep breath, let it out and grabbed the laptop and googled Tiffany Delgado.

Tiffany Delgado lived in Ringgold, Georgia, a dozen miles south of Chattanooga. She was found by her brother Alfonse on Saturday afternoon, August 20, 2019, three years after Franny McNeer's death.

She was thirty-three, single, blonde, five-nine, described as "pretty," and worked as a sales clerk at Rickerton's, a clothing store at the Hamilton Place Mall. She was in her bed. She'd been stabbed thirty-two times. The Catoosa County Coroner's office established the time of death as between eleven o'clock on Friday evening, the 19th, and two in the morning on the 20th. The crime was listed as unsolved.

Mallory sucked on her bottom lip. *It's the same*, she thought. *No wonder Luthor told us to look into it. She was blonde and five-nine. Franny was blonde and five-eight. Same days, same timeline, same method, same rage. Wow! So Luthor's serial killer theory might not be as crazy as we thought. Hmm... How come I never heard of it?*

She googled the *Chattanooga Times* for coverage and found only two small mentions: one on Sunday, August 20th, and the other two weeks later, stating that the investigation into Tiffany Delgado's death was ongoing. The TV coverage was even less, just a passing comment on Channel 7 the following Sunday morning. *Hah, why is that?* she wondered. *And it's been five years. Why is it still unsolved? And why the lack of media coverage? I mean, it's a pretty horrific murder. I would have thought the police would have been all over it.*

She looked at the dog and said, "What d'you think, Annie?"

Annie cocked her head and gazed sleepily up at her. "Yeah," she said dryly. "Me, too." She took a sip of her wine and went back to her computer.

Maybe they were concerned about scaring the community, she thought. *Who knows?* She sucked on her bottom lip, squinted, scratched her head, pursed her lips and slowly shook her head. *This happened five years ago, and it's still unsolved. Wow!*

She picked up her phone and called Tucker.

"Mallory," he said when he picked up. "It's almost eight o'clock. I was just about to take a shower. What is it?"

"I know, I know, and I'm sorry, but I just had to talk to you. I've been researching the Tiffany Delgado case, and I just know they're related. They have to be. They are the same. I mean, exactly the same and—"

"Hey, hey, slow down," he said, interrupting her. "I told you I didn't want to talk about it tonight, that we'd talk about it in the morning. Now, please, stop it. Watch some TV and then go to bed and get a good night's sleep. We'll talk it over in the morning."

"Yes, but—"

"No buts. Get some rest, okay?"

"But, Tucker…" she began again, but it was no use. Tucker had hung up.

"Geez," she snapped and threw the phone down on the couch. "I can't believe him. He's such a—" She cut herself off, folded her arms, pursed her lips and glowered down at the laptop.

Finally, she made an angry face, unfolded her arms,

grabbed her glass and downed the rest of the wine. Then she smacked her lips, stretched her arms above her head, and set the laptop back on the coffee table and leaned back and closed her eyes.

She stayed like that for several minutes, or so she thought. In fact, she woke an hour later with a painful cramp in her right leg, which was curled up underneath her.

"Ouch, ouch, ouch," she muttered as she stood up and flexed her leg.

She looked at her watch. It was two minutes after nine.

"Come on, Annie," she said. "I'll let you out, then I'll get a shower. We'll have an early night. What d'you say?"

Annie said nothing. She just sat there on the couch with her head tilted, looking up at her.

"Yeah, that's what I thought you'd say. Come on. Let's go."

7

THURSDAY, NOVEMBER 21

Mallory woke at six-thirty the following morning to a cold bedroom and a light fog over the backyard.

She put on her robe, tiptoed downstairs, hugging herself, turned the heat up to seventy-three, let Annie out, and then ran back upstairs. She'd showered before going to bed, so she didn't bother to take another. Instead, she washed her face, brushed her teeth vigorously, brushed out her dark blonde hair and tied it back in a ponytail, then dressed in a pair of jeans, a tee shirt and a white lambswool sweater. That done, she glanced at herself in the mirror, made a face, then went downstairs and let Annie back in and fed her. She made herself some scrambled eggs on toast, some coffee, and then sat down to eat it, her laptop open in front of her.

So, she thought as she forked some of the egg into her mouth. *I'll go to work, talk to Tucker and see what we can figure out about Tiffany—and then maybe go talk to Vinnie. Did he know about the Tiffany case, I wonder, and is that why he's pushing so hard—?*

The thought was interrupted by her phone ringing. She picked it up and looked at the screen. It was Tucker. She frowned, then answered it. "Hey, what's up?"

"I'm thinking I'll see if I can talk to Crystal Lawrence, Luthor's daughter. She comes off shift at eight. Do you want to come with me?"

She paused for a second before answering, then said, "No, I don't think so, Tucker. I think I'm going to take Annie to the dogsitter, then head on over to the Ringgold police station and see if I can talk to the detective who worked the Delgado case. That okay with you?"

Where the hell did that come from? she thought as she waited for him to answer.

"Sure," he said, "but please behave yourself. I don't want to have to come and bail you out. What's the address, by the way?"

"Very funny," she said and laughed. "I always behave myself."

"The hell you do," he replied, also laughing. "So where is it? I need to know in case you do get yourself locked up."

"It's in Ringgold," she replied. "I don't have the address yet, but I'll send it to you when I do. Just in case, huh? Tucker, why is it you always think I'm going to cause a stir? You know I never do that!"

"Ah, but you do tend to rub folks the wrong way, especially when they don't cooperate the way you want them to. Please take it easy on those poor cops in Ringgold, okay?"

"Geez, Tucker, you're something else. Okay, I'll be sweet. We'll keep in touch, okay?"

"Yup. Talk to you soon. Good luck."

"Thanks," she replied and hung up.

Geez, she thought, *I had no intention of going without him. Still, it should be fun.* "Right, Annie?"

She finished her breakfast, touched up her makeup, checked the H&K P938 in her shoulder bag, slipped on a tan suit jacket, checked herself one last time in the mirror, and then shrugged. Not wanting to leave Annie home alone all day again, especially knowing she was going to be in and out of the office all day, Mallory took Annie out to the car, loaded her up, and took her to the new doggy daycare that her sister Jen took Tobin to sometimes.

And what's this about Luthor's daughter? she wondered as she drove north on I-24 and bore right onto I-75. *Where did that come from? Luthor never mentioned her. Or did he and I missed it? I don't think so. I wouldn't have missed something like that. Would I? I wonder if Tucker has spoken to Vinnie. Huh. I guess he'll tell me when he wants to. Even so, he could've mentioned it last night when I called him.* And so she continued, one thought after another, coursing rapid fire through her brain until, finally, she pulled into the Ringgold Police Department parking lot.

Oh, Lord, she thought as it dawned on her that she'd never done anything like this before. *What am I going to say?* And, for once in her life, Mallory had no answer. She sat there for a moment, gathering herself and her thoughts together, then made sure she had several of her business cards handy, gritted her teeth, stepped out of the car, and walked confidently into the building.

"Good morning, ma'am. How can I help you?" the receptionist asked.

"Um, yes, good morning. My name's Mallory Carver. I'm a private investigator, and I was hoping I could have a few minutes with the detective who's leading the Tiffany Delgado murder investigation." And then she held her breath as the receptionist looked skeptically at her for a moment, then picked up the phone and punched in a number.

Mallory was terrified. She'd just tried to pass herself off as a PI. *Well, I am, practically...* she thought. *Well, not really. But close enough. I'm working on getting my credentials.*

"Hey, Finn," the receptionist said into the phone. "I have a PI out here wants to talk to you about the Delgado case. Says her name is...?" She looked at Mallory.

"Carver. Mallory Carver," she mouthed.

"Carver. What d'you want me to do with her...? Yeah." She glanced at Mallory, then shrugged and said, "Looks legit to me, but what do I know...? Okay, will do." And she hung up and said, "If you'll take a seat over there, Detective Harper will be with you shortly."

Mallory, her heart fluttering, sat down to wait, her hands clasped together in her lap, and looked around the lobby, noting a woman aged about thirty arguing with a young officer. Actually, it was she who was doing the arguing. She was ranting on and on about how she was being stalked, and they were doing nothing about it.

"This is the fourth time I've been in here, and you're not listening to me." Her voice was loud enough for Mallory to hear what she was saying. "When are you going to do something about it? Are you going to wait until he frickin' rapes me or murders me? What's the matter with you people? What do I have to do before you do something, die?"

"And I keep telling you, Miss Wilson," the detective she was talking to said, "there's not much we can do until—"

"Miss Carver?"

"Yes!" Mallory was startled by the sudden interruption, but she jumped to her feet, clutching her shoulder bag.

"I'm Detective Finn Harper," the young woman said, smiling, trying not to laugh. "If you'd like to come on back, I'll be glad to talk to you."

She followed the detective into a large room with several desks and an overabundance of filing cabinets.

"This is me," Harper said, waving a hand at an overly cluttered desk just to the left of the door. "Please, sit down."

"Thank you for agreeing to see me," Mallory said.

"Not a problem. Marcy, that's the receptionist, said you're a PI. Can I see your credentials, please?"

Oh shit! "I'm afraid this is all I have," and she handed her one of her cards. "I'm still working on them, my credentials. I'm working with Tucker Randall. He's an ex-FBI special agent—"

"I know who he is, and you," she said. "I checked you out while you were waiting for me. Good luck with your exams, Miss Carver. Now, you want to talk to me about the Delgado case? You do know it's five-years cold, right?"

Mallory heaved a sigh of relief, then said, "Yes, I know. But we've been asked to look into what we think could be a related case. It's even colder, but the MO is similar and so is the victim. We haven't yet decided to take it, and I was wondering about... the... Delgado case."

"Go on," Harper said, nodding.

"Okay..." She thought for a moment and then continued, "Franny McNeer was stabbed to death in her bed—"

"Wait, whoa," Harper said, interrupting her. "I know that one. Her husband killed her. Well, he was convicted and sent to prison for it. I spoke to... someone at the sheriff's department. Can't remember who it was, but I can look it up. He said it was open and shut, a slam dunk, that they had him dead to rights."

"That sounds like Kal Cundiff," Mallory said dryly.

"Yeah, that's the one. But you think different?"

"His brother does. He's the one who wants to hire us. We went to Riverbend yesterday and talked to the husband. He claims he's innocent."

"Don't they all?" Harper asked with a smile.

Mallory nodded. "Yes, they do, but I have a feeling this guy might just be telling the truth."

"That's hard to believe, knowing what I know about the case. Didn't he say he slept through it all?"

"He says he did," Mallory replied.

"So, you want to know what I know?" Harper said, locking eyes with her.

She was younger than Mallory, *in her late twenties*, she thought, *but she has an... older way about her.* Mallory nodded and said, "Please."

"Tiffany was murdered in the middle of the night in her bed. She was stabbed thirty-two times. There was no sign of forced entry, and the crime scene was clean... Too clean, considering the method of killing. We had a couple of suspects, but neither of them panned out.

"One, she had a stalker, an ex-boyfriend by the name of Ollie Palmer. I don't think Ollie was responsible... But we've not ruled him out, either.

"Two, we had a second suspect, Raul Copper. He was arrested for wounding a woman, a jogger, in the Prentice Cooper Forest with a hunting knife in 2016 and was sent to prison for three years. He was let out of prison on June 5th, 2019, just two months prior to Tiffany's death. Coincidence? I don't know." She paused and thought for a moment. "Anyway,

I've been keeping an eye on him. He's back in prison, in Tennessee, in Hamilton County jail for aggravated burglary. Look," she continued, "it's still officially an open investigation, but it's growing colder by the day, even with Raul Copper as a suspect. Whoever killed Tiffany must have had a motive, but, as yet, we don't know what it was. She wasn't sexually assaulted, and we've been unable to find anyone who might have had a problem with her. We just don't know. And it couldn't have been McNeer because he was inside."

"No, it couldn't," Mallory agreed, "but Tiffany's killer could have killed Franny McNeer. That's a possibility, right?"

"Of course," Harper agreed.

"And, if that's the case," Mallory said, "and I'm not saying it is, there could be more."

Harper nodded skeptically and said, "So what you're saying is we might have a serial killer on our hands?"

"It would make sense, don't you think?" Mallory asked.

Again, Harper nodded, more slowly this time, then said, "I don't know, and I'm not sure I want to go there, not yet anyway. To go that route would cause a public uproar and my chief wouldn't go for it, anyway. So, let's do this. If you and your partner want to investigate the Delgado case, that's fine with me. I'll help if I can. Give me a moment and I'll have the file copied for you."

Mallory thanked her, and Harper left, leaving her with mixed emotions. She was gone for almost ten minutes before she returned with the copies. But while Mallory was waiting, she had time to think. *Damn, I screwed up. I should have checked to see if there are more similar unsolved murders. That's my next project. I need to call Tucker and tell him what I've found out.*

She fished her phone out of her bag and tapped the speed dial. The phone rang twice and then went to voicemail.

Damn!

"Oh, thank you," she said as she stood up and took the file from Harper. "Look, I'm going to do some research. If I find anything, I'll let you know. In the meantime..." She fumbled around inside her bag, inadvertently giving Harper a glimpse of the P938.

"Nice weapon," she said with a smile.

"What? Oh. Oh yes. It was a gift from Tucker. Um, here's Tucker's card. If you need to get in touch with either of us..."

"Yep, I'll call you," Harper replied.

8

It was a few minutes to eight when Tucker walked into the hospital lobby that morning, hoping to catch Crystal Lawrence as she came off-shift. He checked in at the information desk and asked if she'd left yet and was told she hadn't, so he sat down to wait.

The lobby was quiet; just a few people he figured must be patients and several nurses scurrying back and forth, as nurses usually do. So engrossed in people watching was he that he almost missed the young woman, who barely looked old enough to be a nurse, though he knew her to be in her thirties, step out of the elevator with a large bag over her shoulder and walk quickly to the front entrance.

Tucker rose to his feet, hurried after her, and caught her at the elevators to the parking garage.

"Mrs. Lawrence?"

She stopped, turned around, frowned, and backed away.

"Who are you? What d'you want?"

He stopped some ten feet away from her and held up his hand. "My name's Tucker Randall—"

"Go away. Leave me alone. I don't do interviews." And she turned away.

"No, no!" he said quickly. "That's not why I'm here. I'm a private investigator. I've been hired by your uncle, Vinnie, to look into the death of your mother. Can you spare me just a few minutes, please?"

"Vinnie?" she asked, frowning. "Why would he do that?"

"He thinks your father is innocent. Can we talk?"

She stared at him for a moment, still frowning, then said, "I suppose... but not here. I have to go home and let the dog out. If you want to follow me, we can talk there. My car's in the parking ramp. Where are you?"

"I'll be waiting for you at the exit," Tucker said.

She nodded, turned, and stepped into the elevator. Tucker watched as the doors closed and then went to his car.

Crystal Lawrence was a petite young brunette with brown eyes and a winning smile, though Tucker saw it only once during their conversation. She lived in a small, Cape Cod-style home on Cannondale Loop off Holly Oak Lane off Igou Gap Road.

"Nice place you have here," he said as he looked around the living room.

"Thank you. Please sit down. I'll get us some coffee."

He was about to refuse when he realized it was still only eight-forty-five and decided to go with the flow.

"Me and Jim, we've lived here since just before my mom died," she said as she returned with the coffee. "She used to come visit us. It's been eight years, but I still miss her."

Tucker nodded, then said, "That was quick," as she handed him the cup.

"Coffee pods," she said tiredly. "What did we ever do without them?"

"I wonder that myself sometimes," he lied. "So, Jim is your husband?"

She looked at him as if to say, 'Of course he is. What the hell d'you think I am?'

"Ah, yes, of course he is," Tucker said. "I'm sorry. I didn't mean to infer that—"

"It's all right," she said, cutting him off. "I understand. You're just trying to make conversation. There's no need, and there's no need to apologize. Yes, Jim is my husband and, if you're wondering where he is, he's already gone to work. Now, if you have something to say, please say it."

He nodded, took a sip of his coffee, and said, "Vinnie thinks your father is innocent. I talked to your father yesterday. He insists he's innocent. What do you think?"

"I think he's innocent, too. My father is... was, many things, Mr. Randall, but he's not a murderer, and he loved my mother dearly."

"I find it kind of strange that he never mentioned you," Tucker said.

"That's because we haven't spoken in years," she replied, "even before my mother's death."

"Oh, really? And why is that?"

She took a deep breath, sighed, and looked down at the coffee table that separated them. "My father," she began, "was always... a little crooked... if there is such a thing as a little crooked." She paused, leaned forward, rested her elbows on her knees, and clasped her hands. "He was an accountant, an independent. He was, I think, well, less than honest would be putting it mildly. He worked for some shady people. I know that because I met some of them."

"How did you know they were shady?" Tucker asked.

"Because they were drug dealers," she replied. "And so was

he, though not in a big way, I think, though he certainly was reckless about it. He would go on benders. And he stayed out all night nearly every Friday night... I think he was even seeing prostitutes."

Tucker frowned. This was something new. *Why didn't Vinnie tell me about it?* he wondered.

"Did your mother know about his drug use and...?" he asked.

Crystal shrugged. "I think she probably did. It wasn't a secret. I think my mother condoned it because she had the life she wanted and money to spend."

"On what?" Tucker asked, then thought, *That was a damn silly question.*

Crystal smiled. "Whatever she wanted, of course." But then the smile faded, which Tucker thought was a shame because the smile had lit up her face.

"They were always arguing," she said. "Mostly about money, but isn't that what most married couples do? But I know he loved her. And to stab her forty-three times? No, he was never a violent man; he doesn't have that in him. Now, if you don't mind. I need to shower and then go to the store."

Tucker nodded and rose to his feet. "Just one more question, Mrs. Lawrence. Is there anyone you know of that might have done this?"

She took a deep breath, locked eyes with him and said, "I told you they argued a lot and that it was usually about money, and it was, but that wasn't all they argued about. She was very friendly with one of his clients. Gavin Gray."

Tucker's eyebrows rose. She had his interest.

"Like in an affair friendly?" he asked.

Again, she shrugged. "I don't know. I do know my father

didn't like him, though he did his books and sometimes Gavin paid him with product."

"By product, you mean drugs?"

"Make of it what you will," she replied. "I was only twenty-three at the time and in college, UTC nursing school. I left home when I was nineteen to live on campus. Silly really, when you think about it. But I couldn't stand the constant arguing or my father's activities. If I could have afforded to go farther away, I would have. As it was, I had to wait tables to get through school. My father never helped, though my mother did chip in from time to time. I haven't spoken to my father since."

"That's sad," Tucker said.

"It is what it is," she replied.

"So, where can I find this Gavin Gray?" Tucker asked.

"I'm not sure. Last I heard, he was running the Scarlet Pimpernel—emphasis on the pimp—on Dodd's Avenue. You could try there."

Tucker thanked her, handed her his card, and left her on the front porch, her arms folded across her body, watching him go.

9

Tucker was in the car and about to start the engine when his phone rang. He checked the screen. *Mallory!* He thought as he declined the call. He had every intention of telling Mallory everything he'd learned and to listen to what she'd learned, if anything, but the idea of taking her to a place like the Scarlet Pimpernel... Well, he just didn't feel comfortable about it, even knowing that she'd worked in a bar that might be just as seedy, though sans the strippers, for ten years and thus was hardened to such places. Even so, if he could avoid it, he would, and he did.

It was almost ten o'clock that morning when he strode confidently into the small, low-ceilinged, dimly lit cave-like bar area where a rather lovely, though topless, woman aged about thirty was tending the bar.

Contrary to what you might think, that the place would be deserted at ten o'clock on a weekday morning, there were seven men seated at the small round tables, most of them smoking, all of them watching the all but naked young woman slowly gyrating around a chrome-plated pole. She was, of course, blonde, though from the dark roots it had come from a bottle, and was wearing only a G-string, the tiny scarlet patch of cloth barely covering her... Well, you get the idea.

He stepped up to the bar and asked the topless woman if Gavin Gray was available.

"What you want with him, hun?" she asked, leaning on the bar, her bust flattening on the onyx top.

Tucker smiled at the ploy, nodded in acknowledgment of the obvious show of "talent?" and said, "I just want to talk to him, is all."

"Sure, sweety. If you'll follow me..." And she lifted the hatch, stepped through, and walked toward an even darker opening at the far end of the bar, her hips swaying seductively. Again, Tucker smiled. It was quite a show. She had a knockout figure, that was for sure, and she was wearing only four-inch heels and a micro skirt that left little to the imagination.

She stopped in front of a door at the far end of the dimly lit corridor, turned to face him—she really was stunningly beautiful—and said, "My name is Carly." She lowered her chin, looked at him through her eyelashes, and continued, "If you like what you see, stop by the bar on your way out. I get off at six. It won't cost you a dime."

Then she opened the door and said, "Someone to see you, Gav." Then she walked back toward him, turned sideways and brushed past him, her breasts brushing against his arm. "You'd better go in. He doesn't like to be kept waiting." Then she winked and said, "Not a dime."

He stood for a moment and watched her go. It was quite a performance, and one she'd obviously spent a lot of time practicing.

"Come on in, if you're coming," a voice shouted. "I ain't got all day."

Gavin Gray was much younger than he'd expected, maybe mid-thirties; maybe a little older, but not much. He was seated at his desk, a stocky man with a shaved head and cold, steely blue eyes that even Tucker found a little unnerving. He could see the right-hand desk drawer was open and Gray's hand on the desktop above it.

"You're not going to need that," Tucker said. "I just want to talk."

The steely blue eyes never left his own, but the hand lifted and pushed the drawer closed, and he said, "Who are you, and what d'you want to talk about? And be quick about it. I'm a busy man."

"My name is Tucker Randall, and I'm a private investigator. I want to talk to you about Franny McNeer. Remember her?"

Gray grinned at him. It was more of a snarl than a grin, and there was not a doubt in Tucker's mind that this man was a real badass and wouldn't hesitate to use violence, even deadly force if he thought it was necessary.

"Franny..." Gray said thoughtfully. "Now there's a name I haven't heard in a while. What about her?"

"Did you kill her?" Tucker asked, smiling at him. *Two can play your game*, he thought.

Gray laughed. "Geez," he said. "Why don't you just tell it like it is? What was that about? You trying shock and awe? It won't work, my friend. There's nothing in this world that can shock me. I've seen it all. Two deployments to Afghanistan and this shithole will do that to you. Now, why don't you play nice, and we'll talk?"

"So, what you're saying is that you didn't kill her?" Tucker said quietly.

"No, I didn't kill her, you smart-ass son of a bitch."

"What was your relationship with her?" Tucker asked.

"My relationship was with her husband, Luthor, though…" he blew out a breath, then continued, "She was a great lay. I'll say that for her."

"So, you were having an affair with her?"

"Affair? Hmmm, no! Was I screwing her? Yes! And was I paying well for it? That, too."

"You were paying her?" Tucker frowned. "She was a hooker?"

"Not hardly. I was paying indirectly. I was paying her husband. He was doing my books, and very creatively, I might add. He knew what was going on. The guy loved her, but they weren't doing so good in the bedroom, if you get what I mean." He shrugged. "I think he was kinda grateful I was looking after her, you know? No, it wasn't an affair, but I was very fond of her, in my own way."

Tucker was stunned by the revelation.

"But here's the thing, Mr. PI—is that really a thing, PI, by the way? Ah, never mind. What I was going to say is, they nailed Luthor for it. Big mistake. That man ain't got it in him. I never seen him angry in all the time I knew him. So, if you're looking for the son of a bitch that killed her, good luck to you. I hope you get him."

"What about you and Luthor?" Tucker asked. "He did your books. Was that on the up and up, or did he cause you some grief?"

Ray smiled at that. "Grief? He was a crooked son of a bitch, that's for sure. But, as I said, he was creative. Let's leave it at that. Look, Luthor was a shady character, and he owed me money, a lot of money, but not enough for me to seek retribution. He was always late with his payments, which cost him more than me in vig, but he always paid, eventually. I've known Luthor for a long time, as far back as when his dad was running the business. No, I wouldn't kill him over a few thousand dollars. That's not me. Ten grand, however. That would be a different story." He grinned, showing two rows of perfect, shiny white teeth. It was a scary sight.

"He didn't do it. He didn't kill his wife, Mr. Randall. He wasn't the violent type, and you can take that to the bank; I know that type very well."

"So, if he didn't do it, who d'you think did?"

He made a face, turned down the corners of his mouth, then shook his head and said, "I don't know," he replied. "If I did, I'd tell you. No, I'd kill the bastard myself. I thought a lot of Franny. She didn't deserve to die, not like that. Bless her heart."

Tucker locked eyes with him, nodded slowly, then said, "Thank you for your time, Mr. Gray. I appreciate it. If you think of anything, anything at all."

"Yeah, yeah. I'll call you, but don't hold your breath… Oh, and steer clear of Carly on the way out. She's bad news. Just sayin'." He grinned knowingly at Tucker.

Tucker nodded, smiled at him, rose to his feet, and closed the door behind him. And so, thoughtfully, Tucker returned to his car and called Mallory.

"Hey," he said when she answered. "Sorry I couldn't take your call. I was on my way to… Never mind. I'll fill you in when I see you. Where are you? You want to get some lunch?"

"Perfect. I talked to Detective Harper at Ringgold earlier this morning. She gave me a name, Ollie Palmer, and she gave me a copy of the Delgado file and, get this, I came back to the office and did some research. I have two more names and two more cases... Hey, we are taking Vinnie's case, aren't we—?"

"Mallory, please shut up for just a minute. I know you're excited, and so am I, but I have a headache. Can we just talk about it quietly over lunch? I'll pick you up in fifteen minutes. I'm on Shallowford Road. I need to get gas and something for this headache."

"Well, yes, sure. See you... in a little while, then."

Tucker sighed and shook his head as he hung up. *She's a pistol and I love her to death, but she sure can talk. Yeah, boy, but she's also damn good at what she does. Then why don't you tell her that? Shut the hell up, Tucker. Hah, this is just a few blocks from where Crystal lives. How about that?* He sighed as he turned right onto Gunbarrel and then made a left into the Pitt Stop service station. It was a big, busy enterprise with eight sets of pumps, two service bays and a convenience store.

He pulled up to the pump, sat for a moment, then slid out of the car and filled her up. Then he went into the store to pay and get some aspirin and an energy drink. *And if that isn't a paradox, I don't know what is*, he thought.

He found the energy drinks, picked one out, took it to the counter, and asked for a bottle of aspirin from behind the counter.

The guy behind the counter—wearing a name tag that pronounced him Pete—handed them to him, rang him up, and said, "You know those two don't mix well, right? That energy stuff will tear your guts up."

"Yeah, so they say, but you only live once, and I have a terrible headache."

"Well, I'm telling you, that stuff ain't good for you."

"Yeah, well, my job will likely kill me before it does, but thanks, anyway."

Pete nodded and said, "Take care, and have a good rest of the day."

Tucker nodded and went back to his car. And there he sat for a moment, looking at the energy drink, then he shook his head, opened the car door and tossed it into the trash. *I guess the aspirin will have to wait until I get home*, he thought as he pulled out of the gas station and headed toward East Brainerd Road.

10

It was almost noon when Tucker arrived back at the office to find Mallory printing off information about the other unsolved cases she'd found. She'd already marked the locations on a map on the office wall.

"Hey," she said as he entered the office. "How did it go with Crystal?"

"I'm hungry," he replied, grinning. Oh, how he loved to tease Mallory by making her wait for the information he'd gathered. He considered it part of her professional training to learn patience. "You ready?"

She looked at him and sighed, then said, "Sure. Where would you like to go?"

"How about the Acropolis? It's always good, and it's only ten minutes or so away."

"Okay, but can we talk while we eat?" she asked. "I have a lot to tell you."

"Of course. That was the plan," he replied.

The Acropolis at lunchtime is always busy, but Tucker, who seemed to be well known there, was received with a smile and a nod, and they were shown to a table after only a few minutes' wait.

"Okay," he said after they'd ordered. "I can see you're itching to tell me, so go ahead."

"I'm not itching… Oh, yes. I see. Well, okay." She began by telling him about her visit to the Ringgold police department and her talk with Finn Harper.

"…and she gave me a copy of the Delgado file. But here's the thing, as I was on my way back to my car and I began to wonder how many more women had suffered a fate similar to Franny and Tiffany, and guess what?"

She paused, looking at him expectantly.

"Okay," he said. "I'll bite. What did you find?"

"I found two more, and though they're not quite the same MO, the crimes are similar enough that they might well be connected, and so all four could be the work of a single perpetrator. The two new victims—well, they're not really new. They both died before Franny, but… Their names are Bernice Carr, who was murdered late in the evening on April 15, 2016, and Elaine May, who died in the late evening of July 10, 2015. Both women died late on a Friday evening of multiple stab wounds. Both cases are unsolved. That's four, Tucker. What d'you think?"

"I think you did very well, Mallory," he replied. "However—"

"Oh, come on, Tucker. There's always a however with you. These two murders, three murders, are all connected to Franny's. I just know it."

"All I was going to say," he said, "was that we need to do our due diligence before we go that route."

"I've already done some," Mallory replied. "You want to hear?"

"Of course I do," he said. "But can we eat first?" he asked as the waiter put their food down in front of them.

Mallory sighed, nodded, shook her head and said, "You're such a killjoy sometimes, Tucker."

Tucker simply smiled at her and picked up his fork.

Mallory took a small bite of her salmon, chewed thoughtfully, swallowed, and said, "I've done some preliminary research into both Ollie Palmer and Raul Copper. Palmer was Tiffany's ex-boyfriend, and he'd been stalking her. Copper had been in prison since August 17, 2016, a little more than a month after Franny was murdered, on an unrelated assault charge… with a knife. He was out again on June 7, 2019, two months before Tiffany was murdered. So, there was a three-year gap between when he went to prison and when he got out when there were no murders. As soon as he does, Tiffany is murdered. I think that's pretty compelling. Don't you?"

"I do," he said. "Now eat your lunch before it gets cold."

"Grrrrr," she said.

He grinned at her, then forked another cut of steak into his mouth and chewed slowly.

Finally, over coffee, he told her about his interviews with Crystal Lawrence and Gavin Gray.

"Look," he said when he'd finished, "I agree that Franny and Tiffany *could* have been killed by the same person. The other two? We have a lot of work to do before we can include them. Agreed?"

"Agreed," she said. "So, does this mean we're taking Vinnie's case?"

He nodded. "It does."

"Good," she said, "then let's drop by The Saloon and pick up the cash."

11

Vinnie was, to say the least, excited and handed the envelope containing the cash to Mallory with a smile and a hug.

"Thanks, Mal," he whispered in her ear before releasing her. "I just knew you'd come through for me. How about a drink? Gin and tonic?"

"I know you were, Vinnie," she replied. "We think he's innocent, too, but proving it is going to be hard, and this," she said, waving the envelope in the air, "might not be enough."

He turned the corners of his mouth down and nodded. "Not a problem, Mal. I've been saving everything I've earned from the bar ever since they arrested him. I've got money. That ten grand is just a retainer. I know that. You guys do what you gotta do. I'll pay whatever you ask, and if I run out, I'll take out a loan. Now, how about that drink?"

Mallory looked at Tucker. He nodded. "I'll have a Modello," he said. "Thanks, Vinnie."

Vinnie nodded, went back behind the bar and made the drinks and beer for himself.

It was a given that Vinnie wanted to talk about the case.

They filled him in on their progress as best they could without giving too much away, and by the time they'd answered all his questions, it was well after four o'clock.

"I have to go pick up Annie," Mallory said, looking at her watch. She stood up, went around the table, bent down and kissed Vinnie on the forehead. "We'll be in touch, Vinnie. Come on, Tucker."

Ninety minutes later, after Annie had been fed, and a pizza had been delivered and half-eaten, Mallory had showered and was in her pajamas, but she wasn't done for the day; she still had work to do, be it self-imposed.

She came downstairs, went to the kitchen, made herself a large mug of hot chocolate, then went to the living room, ordered Annie up onto the couch and opened her laptop. Then she sat there for a moment, looking at the lock screen and wondering where to begin.

Finally, after another moment of indecision, she googled Elaine May and was rewarded with several painfully brief articles.

The first was published in the *Chattanooga Times* on Sunday, July 12, 2015. It was the early coverage, if you could call it that, of the murder and a statement by the Cleveland, Tennessee, Police Chief, Otis Woody. The article was short and sparse on detail, saying not much more than Elaine May, aged thirty-two, had been found dead in her home on Spring Place Road. The cause of death? Multiple stab wounds. The police chief had little more to say other than the investigation was ongoing and that he would not answer questions.

The *Cleveland Daily Banner* article dated the same day was equally scant on detail. They were the same articles Mallory had found when she'd done her research earlier that day. The TV hadn't covered it at all. And Mallory wondered why.

And it was the same with Bernice Carr, aged thirty-six of Meigs County, Tennessee. She died in her home off Highway 30 in Decatur on Friday evening, April 15, 2016, also of multiple stab wounds. Again, there was little media coverage and, again, Mallory wondered why not.

What she did notice was that each victim had lived in a different county, but none in Hamilton County or the city of Chattanooga. *Which,* she thought, *probably accounts for the lack of coverage here. Hmm, we've talked to Ringgold, and Detective Harper was helpful, which was unexpected. And to Kevin Cundiff, who was reluctantly helpful. Now we need to talk to Cleveland and Decatur... hmm... I wonder?* She looked at her watch. It was just after six-forty-five. "Hah, can't hurt to try, can it?" she muttered and picked up her phone and asked Siri to connect her to the Cleveland Police Department.

"Cleveland Police," a female voice said.

"Oh, hi, er, hello," Mallory stuttered. "My name is Mallory Carver. I'm a private investigator and I was hoping to speak with the lead detective on the Elaine May case."

"The who case?" Mallory could almost see the frown.

"Elaine May. She was murdered in Cleveland on July 10, 2015."

There was a moment of silence, then, "Hold on, I'm transferring you to Serious Crimes."

There was another brief silence and then, "Detective Foley!"

"Oh, yes, thank you," Mallory began. "I'm Mallory Carver,

and I was wondering if I could speak with the detective who's investigating the Elaine May murder."

"That would be... no one," Foley said after a brief pause. "That case went cold four years ago. Why are you interested now?"

"We, that is my managing partner, Randall Tucker—" She closed her eyes and shook her head. "We're investigating what we think might be a related case, and I thought, after having done some research, that the Elaine May case might also be connected... somehow. So if I could talk to.... Oh, hell. Look, I just want some details. The media coverage was all but nonexistent. I know she was killed late on a Friday evening and that she died of multiple stab wounds. Those two details gel with our case, but I need more. So, can I talk to him, or her, please?"

"You're new to the job, aren't you?" Foley said.

Oh geez, here we go, she thought. "No, not really."

"Come on. Tell me," Foley said, sounding as if he was laughing. "How long have you been a PI? I can tell you were never a cop. You sure you're not just some idiot reporter trying to pull a fast one? If you are, you can forget it."

"I'm the junior partner in Randall & Carver Private Investigations," she replied haughtily. "We're investigating the 2016 murder of Franny McNeer of Greasy Creek, Polk County. Now, if you want to call my partner, Tucker Randall, I can give you his number."

"You still didn't tell me how long you've been a PI," he said.

Now she was sure he was laughing at her.

She took a deep breath and said, "I'm not. I'm still working to get my credentials."

"Hah, I thought so," he said. "I'm Edward Foley. The May

case was mine. I closed it out unsolved four years ago. So, where are you?"

"East Chattanooga, why?"

"I was just wondering. Go ahead. Ask your questions. I'll tell you what I can on the understanding that it's off the record and not for publication."

"Well, I know she was stabbed to death, but what else can you tell me?"

"Okay. Let's see. The time of death was, according to the ME, sometime between ten on Friday night and two in the morning. She was stabbed thirty-seven times in the upper torso with a large knife, probably a hunting knife, but we don't know for sure. It wasn't found at the scene. The perp broke in through the back door. That help?"

"Yes. Thanks. And she was in bed?" Mallory asked.

"No, she was on the couch in the living room."

"Oh," Mallory said, sounding disappointed.

"That a problem?" Foley asked.

"Well, yes, and no. My victim was in bed. She was stabbed forty-three times. And we have another potential victim in Ringgold. She was also in bed, and she was stabbed thirty-two times. The fact that your victim was on the couch is a break in the pattern."

"Oh, I wouldn't say that," Foley said. "You're nitpicking the details. Look, you already have two similar killings, and now you have mine, also similar, but for one minor detail. Do we have a serial killer? I would tend to doubt it. But three similar killings, all within fifty miles of one another... A coincidence? Maybe, maybe not."

Mallory was encouraged. "How old was Elaine?"

"Thirty-two."

"And she was blonde, I suppose?"

"Yup, and she was a hooker."

"Oh, wow," Mallory said. "How about the crime scene?" she asked. "Did you find anything, hair, fiber, DNA?"

"A lot of blood, some bloody shoe prints. Otherwise, the place was clean, maybe too clean."

"How about suspects?" she asked.

"Just the one," he replied. "One of her regular clients, Morris Watson. Part-time drug dealer, some-time user, and full-time nasty piece of work. We had him in here twice. One time overnight, but nothing came of it."

"Is he worth talking to?" she asked.

"Possibly," he replied. "Couldn't hurt; a fresh face, and all that. Look, tell you what. I'll have the file copied and FedEx it to you tomorrow, unless you'd like to come and pick it up."

"FedEx will be fine. We'll pick up the cost. Thank you, Detective. You've been most kind."

"No problem. I'd like to see the thing closed. Elaine was… she wasn't a bad person. She was just trying to make it, you know?"

"I do," Mallory replied. "Have a good night, Detective."

"You, too, *detective*," he replied, then laughed and hung up.

Mallory blew out a deep breath, lay back against the couch, and closed her eyes. *That's three*, she thought. *Three, and possibly four. I think I'll go to Decatur tomorrow morning.*

But Tucker had other plans.

12

FRIDAY, NOVEMBER 22

Tucker rose early the following morning. Not by design, but because he couldn't sleep. He'd been lying awake since four, his mind in a whirl. His was essentially a one-case-at-a-time business. His resignation from the FBI had thrown him into an emotional vortex of lethargy and indifference. He was only thirty when he resigned after eighteen-year-old Marsha Cline had been murdered by the perp because of a bad call by his AIC, David Lewis. Now, four years on, there wasn't a night he didn't replay that last scene. But that wasn't what was keeping him awake. It was the fragility of his business.

Over the past year, he'd come to rely on Mallory for her insight, intuition and her ability to analyze a given situation almost instantly, not to mention her organizational skills. And the fact that she was a beautiful woman didn't hurt either. But what bothered him was what he perceived as the instability of his business. He wasn't short of money. His father, a respected entrepreneur in the field of electronics, had been killed in a car accident and had left Tucker, his brother and his mother more than comfortably off.

No, the continued success of his business was predicated on his continued ability to find new, well-paying clients, and those, locally, were almost as rare as the proverbial hen's teeth. That, and his responsibility to Mallory and her livelihood, was what kept him awake at night. As a loner with just a part-time secretary, he'd been able to pick and choose his cases practically anywhere in the world, but things were different now, and it bothered him.

So, he finally rose that morning at six feeling as if he hadn't slept at all, showered, felt somewhat better, dressed in jeans and a white dress shirt, then went downstairs and made a pot of coffee, all the time thinking about Mallory. Not anything in particular, just a flurry of random thoughts, some of which gave him a weird feeling in the pit of his stomach, almost as if he was crossing some sort of imaginary line.

But, by seven, he'd put such thoughts out of his head and was in his office, cup in hand, staring at the whiteboard and the images thereon.

At seven thirty, his phone rang. He frowned and picked it up. It was Mallory.

"Hey," he said. "Is something wrong?"

"Huh? What? No, of course not. I was just calling to say I wouldn't be in this morning. I'm going to Decatur to—"

"No, no, no," Tucker interrupted her. "I want you to come with me to interview Raul Copper."

"But, Tucker, I called the Cleveland police last night and talked to the detective about Elaine May. It's the same. That's three, all connected. We have a serial killer, and if I can connect—"

"Whoa, slow down," Tucker said. "We need to talk about

this. You can't go off half-cocked on your own. You come in here. We'll go and talk to Copper, and while we're at it, you can fill me in on what you've found."

He heard her sigh, then she said, "Oh, very well, but I think we can cover more ground if we split up."

"What's the hurry, Mallory?" he asked. "A thorough investigation is a marathon, not a sprint. Now, I'm hungry. D'you want to stop by Hardee's and get us something, or would you like me to make some waffles?"

"Grrrr, I'll stop by Hardee's. What would you like?"

"A sausage and egg biscuit would be nice. I have coffee made. How long will you be?"

"Oh, I'm ready. I just have to drop Annie off. Say... thirty minutes?"

She arrived thirty-five minutes later at eight-fifteen, and they sat together at Tucker's kitchen table and ate their food almost in silence, something Mallory wasn't noted for.

She's sulking, he thought and smiled at her.

"What?" she asked, her biscuit halfway to her mouth.

"You're quiet this morning," he replied. "That's not like you."

She shrugged, then put her biscuit down and said, "On the way here, I thought about what you said, about it being a marathon and not a sprint. You're right. I'm sorry. I've always been a little..."

"Impetuous?" he finished for her.

"Yeah, that, I suppose, or enthusiastic. I just like to get things done, you know?"

"I do, but we need order, purpose, and clarity. We need to identify what must be done and then prioritize. Things are piling up, Mallory. If we don't get a grip on them, they'll overwhelm us. You have two more, possibly connected, cases and we now have a half-dozen possible suspects. You want to go off on your own, but while I respect your enthusiasm, you can't do it like that. We're a team. We need to get our priorities down and tackle them in order. If not... all we'll achieve is chaos."

"Wow," she said. "That's not quite what I expected. I don't know what to say."

"What we're going to do is go to the whiteboard," he said, "and try to put things in some sort of order. I've made a start, but we need to add what you've found out about the May victim."

It was a little after ten-thirty when they took a step away from the whiteboard and stared at it. Two-thirds of it was covered with photographs, names, dates, and notes, including the pertinent details of the Elaine May case and the name Morris Watson, May's client suspect. The remaining third had a list of things they needed to do. Mallory had taken what Tucker had said to heart and had organized the list in order of priority. At the top of the list was: Interview Raul Copper.

"You're sure?" Tucker asked. "You didn't put it at the top of the list just because I said so?"

"No," she replied. "Copper's in Silverdale, the county jail. It's only ten minutes from here, so we don't have to go hunting for him. It makes sense. I'll make the call and see if we can get in to see him."

"There you go," Tucker said, grinning at her.

"Yeah, yeah," she grumbled and then asked Siri to connect her with Silverdale. It took only a few minutes to make an appointment for two-thirty that afternoon.

"Good," Tucker said. "Now. Next on the list is Ollie Palmer, Delgado's ex-boyfriend and stalker. Fire up that computer of yours and see what you can find out about him. Geez, I wish I had access… too… Hmm, I wonder."

"You wonder what?"

"Never mind," he said, thinking better of it. "There should be an address in the file that detective gave you. Her name was Harper, wasn't it?"

"Yeah, I think there is. And there's also Morris Watson," she said. "Detective Foley said he was one of Elaine May's regular clients, and that he's a drug dealer and a user. He also said he was a nasty piece of work, so we need to talk to him, too, right?"

Tucker nodded thoughtfully, his hand to his chin as he stared at the board.

"But before Morris…" she continued, pointing at the list. "And, I know you're not going to like this, but we also need to go to Decatur, to the sheriff's department, ASAP, and talk to the police there about the Bernice Carr murder. I think it's connected."

"Okay," Tucker said after some thought. "We'll run up there tomorrow. There, does that make you happy?"

She grinned at him. "It does."

She stepped over to the map and inserted pins depicting the two new cases, one in Cleveland and one in Decatur, then stood back and said, "There's something weird about this, and I'm not seeing it. Oh well, it will come to me, I guess." She turned to look at Tucker and said, "It's almost twelve. We've got some time. I'll see what I can find on Palmer."

———

Tucker, though he said nothing about it to Mallory, had serious doubts about their interview with Raul Copper. From the little he knew about him, he'd come to the conclusion that he was a hard case, and hard cases were always difficult to deal with. This man had attacked someone, a jogger, in the forest and severely wounded her with a knife. The knife, the young woman; they were tenuous links to the Franny McNeer and Tiffany Delgado crimes, and Tucker was skeptical. *Yes, the timeline's right, but if Copper's a serial killer, why did he leave her alive? But it's also true there was no sexual assault. And as Mallory pointed out, it's also true in the Franny McNeer and Tiffany Delgado cases. But what does that mean, if anything?* Tucker wondered as he turned left off Standifer Gap Road and left again into the parking lot of the Silverdale Detention Facility.

"Are you going to talk to me or not?" Mallory asked as he opened his door.

"What?" he asked, frowning.

"Tucker, where is your head?" she asked. "You've barely said a word to me since we got in the car."

"Well," he said, smiling. "You, my dear, have said enough for both of us."

"What's that supposed to mean?" she asked indignantly as she closed her door and stepped around the front of the car to meet him.

"It means nothing," he replied. "Well, not exactly nothing. I mean, you do talk a lot, and, well… you talk a lot."

"I do not… Do I?" she asked, frowning, as they approached the main entrance.

Tucker didn't answer. He just smiled at her and raised his eyebrows.

"I do not," she muttered as they waited.

"Do, too," he whispered, grinning.

She was about to respond again when a corrections officer in a blue uniform stepped into the room and, without a word, beckoned for them to follow him. And they did, to a small interview room with a steel table and four chairs where dour-looking Raul Copper was already waiting for them.

"Who the hell are you?" he snarled, looking up at them, his elbows on the table.

He was, Tucker knew, forty-two and had spent most of those years in one prison or another. His hair was mousy brown. His face was heavily lined with a scar above his left eye that lifted the outer corner of the eye and gave him a look that was more than a little unnerving.

Tucker looked at the officer, nodded, and said, "You can remove the cuffs."

"You sure? This man is—"

"I'm sure," Tucker said. "Take them off, please."

"Okay, but… Ah, what the hell." And took off the cuffs, backed out of the room, and closed the door.

"I said, who the hell are you?" Copper repeated, rubbing his wrists.

"My name's Tucker Randall. I'm a private investigator, and this is my associate, Mallory Carver."

Copper looked at Mallory, did a double-take, and then slowly rose to his feet. "Pleased to meet you, ma'am," he said, offering her his hand.

She looked at it for a long moment, then reached out and took it.

His grip appeared gentle at first. Then, when she tried to take her hand back, Tucker saw that he tightened it and held on, grinning at her.

"Please," she said, as calmly as she could, "let go."

Tucker made a sound in his throat and leaned toward the man.

Copper stuck out his chin and narrowed his eyes. The quirky look turned sinister, but then he smiled, nodded, let go, and sat down.

"So," he said, looking at Tucker, "you're PI's. What d'you want with me?"

"What can you tell me about Franny McNeer?" Tucker asked.

"Who?" he said, frowning.

"Franny McNeer," Tucker repeated. "She was murdered in her bedroom. She was stabbed forty-three times."

He grinned at him and said, "And you think I had something to do with it?"

Tucker shrugged, already realizing he was on shaky ground. "It would make sense," he said. "The timing's right. You're in here for a similar crime."

Copper stuck out his chin, rubbed it with the fingers of his left hand, and then said, "You're kidding me, right? Look, I know why you're here. It's about that silly bitch I cut in Prentice Cooper. Well, you've got me wrong, pal. I didn't hurt her but a scratch, and she asked for it, anyway. Me and Jimmy Bond was out hunting, see? We was on the trail and she comes running up, spots us, and pulls out a frickin' knife, and then she gets all mouthy, calling us names, like. So me, I just steps up and takes it away from her, before she can hurt someone, see? Well, that ain't good enough for her. She tries to take it back, and that's when she got... hurt."

"She got hurt?" Tucker said. "She had a six-inch gash to her upper arm, and where was this Bond guy while all this was going down? How come he didn't testify for you?"

"I told you, it was an accident. Jimmy was off takin' a leak.

By the time he come back, she was gone. He didn't see nothing."

"They found the knife on you," Tucker said.

"Well, I wasn't going to throw it away, now was I? It was a nice knife, a Kershaw switchblade."

"She testified that she'd never seen it before," Tucker persisted.

"Well, she would, wouldn't she?" Copper replied, leaning back in his chair and folding his arms, and said, "And as to this... Franny woman, I don't know nothin' about her. I done a lot of bad things, but I ain't never killed no one."

Inwardly, Tucker shook his head, then said, "How about Tiffany Delgado?"

Copper stared at him for a long moment, then said, "Never heard of her."

Tucker then mentioned Bernice Carr and Elaine May, already knowing what the answer would be, so he wasn't surprised when Copper said he'd never heard of either of them.

And, for some strange reason he couldn't explain, Tucker believed him.

Tucker looked at Mallory. She nodded and was about to rise to her feet when Copper said, "You're not leavin', are you? I ain't got to talk to the pretty lady yet. She ain't said not one word to me."

Mallory got up, smiled at him and said, "Goodbye, Mr. Copper."

"Well, now, that just ain't neighborly, now is it?"

She ignored him. Tucker knocked on the door. It opened and they left him sitting there, trying unsuccessfully to look outraged.

"He didn't do any of it," she said as they walked back to the car.

"I agree," Tucker said. "It was a total waste of time."

"Well, you knew it would be," she said. "So why do it?"

"Because…" he said. "We have to cover all the bases. So, now that's out of the way, what we have left is Tiffany's stalker, Ollie Palmer, and the Meigs County Sheriff's Department. It shouldn't be too much trouble to find Palmer. You can do that, right?"

She nodded. "I can, and I have the file Detective Foley FedExed to us, so I can work on that, too. If that's okay with you."

"Yes, that's fine," he replied. Then, after a moment's thought, he said, "Look, I have something I need to do, and it's going to take a while, so I suggest you go home, take the files with you, if you want, find out where Palmer lives, or works, and we'll go talk to him first thing Monday morning."

"But, Tucker, what about Decatur—?"

"Yes, I know, and we'll get there, I promise; but for now, I have other things on my mind."

"But what could be more—?"

Again, he cut her off, saying, "Okay, look. If you must know, I have a doctor's appointment at four-thirty this afternoon. And there's someone I need to see tomorrow. My brother's stopping off on his way back to Tulsa. I don't get to see him very often, so…"

"You have a doctor's appointment?" she asked. "What? Why? Is something wrong with you?"

"I have… I have… I have an ulcer, okay? And I need to go now, or I'll be late."

"Oh… Well… Okay, I guess," she said. "I'll see you Monday morning then. You're sure there's nothing else I can do?"

"No. I've got it. I just need to... I'll see you on Monday morning, and we'll go see Palmer. Then, depending on how that goes, we'll figure out what to do next. That sound good?"

"I guess. If you say so," she replied grumpily.

13

MONDAY, NOVEMBER 25

The weekend passed slowly and uneventfully for Mallory. She spent most of her time going through the files and her notes. She also took Annie for long walks through the fields and woods at the rear of her property and, by Sunday afternoon, she was thoroughly bored. Bored enough to drag herself out and go visit her sister Jennifer.

But, as always, Jen was busy, even on Sunday, and her niece, Jackie, was out with her boyfriend. So, the visit was brief. It lasted no more than an hour, and Mallory left feeling just a little hurt, unwanted, and very much out of place.

And so she went back to her little house, let Annie out for a moment, made herself a grilled cheese sandwich, opened a bottle of Pinot Grigio and, together, she and Annie went to the living room. She turned on the TV, sat down on her couch, and took a very man-sized swallow of the wine.

For twenty minutes she flipped through the cable channels, trying to find something that might stop her mind from collapsing completely, until she happened upon the movie *Outlaws and Angels*. It turned out to be an exceedingly graphic, and at times bloody, western. Even so, before it was halfway through, she managed to fall asleep with Annie cuddled on her lap.

———

This Ollie Palmer is one creepy guy, was all Mallory could think when they met him that Monday morning. He was working as a mechanic at an auto repair shop on Rossville Boulevard.

Over the weekend, Tucker had an FBI buddy look him up only to find that, other than a stalking complaint, he had a clean record; and the complaint? It was lodged by Tiffany Delgado.

Tiny's Auto Repair and Service was one of a dozen of its kind on the long strip that was Rossville Boulevard, and it was typical of the genre: a onetime tire shop with three service bays and a small office.

Having left Annie in Tucker's office, Mallory had decided she needed to be in control and so had opted to drive her CRV, much to Tucker's displeasure. Be that as it may, Mallory drove and Tucker sat beside her, biting his tongue until she pulled into Tiny's lot and parked in front of the office.

Tiny Garcia—real name Manuel—was indeed a small man. Only five-six, stocky with black hair, a swarthy face and heavy black eyebrows, he was seated behind his battered steel desk whereon were several heavy tomes, some open, some closed, that Mallory assumed to be service manuals. Tiny was a busy man, as was evidenced by the service bays. All three were full.

"Hey," he said when they entered. "What can I do for you?"

"We'd like to talk to Mr. Palmer," Tucker said. "He's one of your mechanics."

Tiny's eyes narrowed; his brow furrowed. He leaned back in his chair, stared at them, then said, "You want to talk to Ollie? What for? You cops, or what?"

"No, we're not police. It's... a private matter," Tucker replied.

"He's busy," Tiny snapped, leaning forward again. "He gets lunch at eleven-thirty. You come back then."

Tucker nodded slowly and was about to leave when Mallory said, "When was your last OSHA inspection, Mr. Garcia?"

Tiny frowned. "Why you ask that?"

"Well, for one, that large oil spill on your forecourt, and I'm sure that's not the only EPA violation they would find, should an inspection become necessary. Oh, and how many illegals d'you have working here? I'm sure ICE would be pleased to know."

The frown deepened. "You would do that?" he asked.

She shrugged and smiled sweetly at him. "Fifteen minutes with Mr. Palmer, please?" she asked. "In private."

He thought for a moment, the corners of his mouth turned down, his head bobbing from side to side.

"Okay," he said finally, rising to his feet. "I'll go get him. Fifteen minutes. No more. He has work to do."

"Thank you, Mr. Garcia," Mallory said, smiling at him.

Ollie Palmer was everything Mallory hated in a man, and from the moment he set foot in the office, she took a virulent dislike to him. He was tall, a little over six feet, well built, muscular, wearing oil-stained jeans, a plaid shirt with the sleeves cut off at the shoulders, open all the way showing a barrel-like chest covered in a thick matt of hair. His waist was tiny by comparison, and his upper arms were huge, and, from the way he eyed Mallory, he fancied himself as a lady's man.

Tiny ushered him in, then left, closing the door behind him.

"What's this about, then?" he asked, still leering at Mallory. His gaze was penetrating, and Mallory had the distinct feeling he was mentally stripping her of her clothes, one by one.

"My name's Randall. I'm a private investigator. That's my associate, Ms. Carver. It's about Tiffany Delgado," Tucker said, sitting down behind Tiny's desk, leaving Mallory with no option but to take the seat beside Palmer, and she glared angrily at Tucker across the desk.

"You're PI's? I thought you were cops. I don't have to talk to you." He grinned, rising to his feet.

"Sit down, Ollie," Tucker said tiredly. "No, you don't have to talk to us, but if you don't, that will look bad, and you will have to talk to Detective Harper. Remember her?"

He sank slowly back down onto his seat, stared at Tucker, then said, "What about Tiffany?" he asked.

"Well, you and she were an item," Mallory said before Tucker could speak.

He twisted in his chair and looked at her, his eyes narrowed, a half-smile on his lips. "So?" he said softly and licked his lips.

Inwardly, Mallory shuddered. "So, she dumped you and you decided to stalk her," Mallory said. "Did you kill her, Mr. Palmer?"

She saw Tucker roll his eyes. Palmer didn't. He was focused on Mallory.

"What the... Are you serious...? Shit, this ain't happening, lady. I have an alibi. Harper checked it out, and she cleared me."

"That's not what she told me," Mallory retorted. "She told me you're still a person of interest."

"Did she, now?" He was beginning to look worried. "Look, you can't hang that on me. I was at the Billiard Club on Cherry Street till almost one in the morning. You can check it out. I won big that night. No, I didn't kill Tiffany. I loved her. And I wasn't stalking her. I just wanted to talk to her, is all. I would never have hurt her."

There was no other argument Mallory could think of. *If his alibi checks out...* she thought, then said, "What about Franny McNeer?"

"Who?" He looked genuinely puzzled.

"Franny McNeer," she repeated. "Lived in Greasy Creek in Polk County."

"Never heard of her, or it. Greasy Creek? Is that really a place?"

She ignored the question and said, "How about Bernice Carr and Elaine May?"

He slowly shook his head and then said, "Nope. Never heard of either of them."

"Is there anyone, anyone at all, you can think of that might have killed Tiffany or would have wanted to hurt her?" Mallory asked, feeling more than a little frustrated.

"No, missy," he replied. "If there was, I would have told Detective Harper. Tiff was a great gal, sweet as can be. Everybody loved her. I loved her. I don't know nobody as would've wanted to hurt her. If I had, they would've had to deal with me. Maybe it was my fault she got killed. I screwed up, and she finished with me. If we'd still been together, maybe she'd still be alive. Now, we done here? I need to get back to work."

"Yes, we're done," Tucker said, rising to his feet. Thanks for your time, Mr. Palmer."

Palmer also rose to his feet, as did Mallory. He turned to her and offered her his hand.

She took it. His grip was surprisingly gentle.

"Thank you, Mr. Palmer," she said as he released her hand.

"You're welcome, missy. Sorry I couldn't be more help. There's nothing more in the world I'd like to see than the son of a bitch who did it fry." He looked into her eyes, then said, "I don't suppose you'd... Nah, course you wouldn't." And with that, he spun away and walked out the door.

———

"Well," she said when they were back in the car. "I think we can write that one off. What d'you think, Tucker?"

Tucker shrugged. "He seemed pretty up front to me."

"D'you think it's worth checking his alibi?" she asked as she started the engine.

"I think your friend Detective Harper already did that, so there's not much point."

"Are you all right, Tucker? You seem a little off."

"Eh, I'm fine. It's just that... Well, we seem to be at a dead end."

"But we still have Decatur—"

"I have a feeling that's going to be a wash, too," he replied. "We're missing something here, Mal. I think you're right, though, that all four cases may well be connected; but whoever this killer is, he's smart. The three crime scenes we have so far—we don't yet know about Decatur—were clean. He didn't leave a trace. He covered his tracks, and now, so it seems, he's gone to ground."

"So, what do we do?" she asked as she pulled out of Tiny's lot onto Rossville Boulevard.

"I don't know," he replied. "We've agreed it's not Raul Copper, Gavin Gray or Palmer."

"I think we should go to Decatur and talk to the detective who investigated the case."

"Let's go get some lunch," he said. "I'm hungry. We can talk about it some more, but I… I dunno, Mal."

As it turned out, when they got back to the office, Tucker received a phone call from a client about an open case, and they spent the rest of the day dealing with that.

It was almost six that evening when Mallory and Annie left to go home.

Tucker, not feeling particularly hopeful about the McNeer case, spent the next two hours going over the three case files. And while he had to admit to himself that all four cases, including the one in Decatur, had to be connected, he still felt there was something he was missing. What it was continued to elude him until, finally, sometime between nine and ten, he fell asleep on the couch.

14

SATURDAY MORNING, DECEMBER 7

And then the case went cold. For almost two weeks, there was
little they could do but cover old ground. They interviewed
Lieutenant Warner at the Meigs County Sheriff's Department,
the lead detective on the Bernice Carr case, but he was less
than cooperative and seemed to resent the intrusion into
what he considered his personal fiefdom. He refused to
provide any new information or turn over the files. None of
this surprised Tucker. Meigs was, after all, a sparsely popu-
lated rural county with a small sheriff's department
comprising a half-dozen deputies and two detectives.
Mallory, however, couldn't believe Warner's attitude, and she
told him so, at which point Warner ended the interview and
sent them on their way with a warning to stay out of his
investigation.

It wasn't until almost two weeks later, on Saturday,
December 7, that things took a turn for the worse, or better,

depending upon your point of view, when Tucker, who was eating breakfast, was startled by a thunderous knocking at the front door.

What the hell? he thought as he rose from the kitchen table and went to the door. Barely had he unlocked it when it burst open to reveal Mallory in a state of... excitement.

"Look. Here." Her voice was squeaky, excited. She shoved an iPad in front of his face. "It's the local news at eight o'clock this morning. I recorded it. D'you have coffee? You do. Good. I need some." She handed him the iPad and left him standing there in a state of bewilderment.

"I know her," she said as she poured herself some coffee. "You want me to top that up?" She didn't wait for an answer. She grabbed his cup and filled it almost to overflowing, all the while chattering nonstop. "When I say I know her, I should have said I knew her, but not really. She was at the Ringgold Police Department when I was there to interview Detective Harper. She was telling some detective she was being stalked and complaining about how they were doing nothing about it. I didn't get to hear it all because they came and got me, but I did hear the detective say there was nothing they could do about it. I was going to tell you about it, but it went clear out of my mind. And, anyway, now she's dead, murdered, stabbed multiple times. It has to be connected, Tucker. It just has to be."

She sat down at the table opposite him, took her cup in both hands, placed her elbows on the table, took a sip of her coffee, and then stared at him over the rim of the cup.

He looked at her, slowly shaking his head in wonder at his partner's obvious enthusiasm. Her blonde hair was hanging loosely around her face. She was wearing little makeup, just some lipstick and a little blush, but her blue eyes were sparkling, and he thought, not for the first time, how lovely she was, especially when she was excited.

He took a sip from the over-filled cup, replaced it on the table and reran the news piece. There wasn't much to it. The police rarely released details this early in an investigation. All it said was that Holly Wilson, a resident of Ringgold, had been found dead early that morning in her home and that they were treating it as a suspicious death. In a hesitated response to a reporter's question, Detective Finn Harper admitted that Wilson had been stabbed multiple times, and that was all she could say at that time.

"Could it be Ollie Palmer?" Mallory asked, still nursing her cup in front of her face. "He kind of admitted he was stalking Tiffany."

"And he had an alibi for Tiffany's murder," Tucker countered. "So, no."

"Well, Tiffany could have had two stalkers," Mallory insisted. "I know it sounds kind of crazy, but it's not. It happens. I think we should talk to Detective Harper. Look, Tucker. I saw what happened when she tried to get help. They practically blew her off. She was obviously being stalked. Does Harper even know that? Probably not. She needs to know. We need to tell her."

"Take it easy, Mal," Tucker replied. "I'm sure it's just some sort of coincidence. Are you sure the woman you saw was Holly Wilson?"

"The detective called her Miss Wilson, but—"

"But," Tucker said, cutting her off. "Wilson is a common name. We don't even know if it's the same woman. Where's Annie, by the way?"

"She's at day care. I dropped her off. So, are we going to talk to Detective Harper or not?"

Tucker looked at her for a long moment, then, having realized he was fighting a losing battle, sighed, nodded, and said, "Can I finish my breakfast first?"

15

SATURDAY MORNING, DECEMBER 7

11AM HOLLY WILSON

Geez, what are we getting ourselves into? Tucker thought as he turned onto I-75, heading south toward Ringgold. *Mallory, bless her, still doesn't get it. We're just a couple of PIs—one, really— and we just don't have the resources for this kind of major investigation. Two states and four counties... geez. And Mallory seems to have it in her head that we're going to be of great service to everyone, but we've already found in Decatur that we're regarded as nothing more than a nuisance. It's exactly how I would have felt— did feel—when I was an agent. Hell, we don't have even the basic resources, like forensics, IT, much less personnel. Sheesh, this is ridiculous.*

He turned his head to look at her and could see she was deep in thought.

"Hey," he said. "What's going on in that pretty little head?"

She looked at him, shocked. It was the first time he'd ever said anything like that to her, and she didn't quite know what to make of it. Was he making fun of her or was it something else?

"What did you say?" she asked, frowning.

"Yep, sorry. I didn't mean anything by it. I was just trying to make conversation... I'm not taking it back, though," he finished with a grin.

Mallory felt herself blushing. She looked quickly away and pursed her lips to stop herself from smiling.

"I was just thinking," she said, finally.

"About what?"

She shrugged. "Nothing, really. Just... you know... stuff."

"What kind of stuff?"

"Oh, I don't know. Stop it, Tucker. You're being weird."

"Me? Weird?" He turned his head to look at her, smiling. "Isn't that a little like the pot calling the kettle black?"

"Tsk," she said. "I never did understand that silly saying. I've never seen a black pot or kettle."

"Of course you haven't," Tucker said. "You're far too young. It goes back to the time when pots and kettles were heated over an open fire and were covered in soot."

"Well, just listen to Mr. Wikipedia," she retorted, smiling.

He grinned at her but didn't reply.

"So, Tucker," she said. "What do *you* think about... all this... mess?"

He nodded, then said, "So you think it's a mess, too."

"Well, not a mess, exactly, but... well... you know?"

"I do know," he replied, "and it *is* a mess, a real mess. Our case is Luthor McNeer, but here we are in the midst of what's beginning to look like an interstate investigation we have no business being involved in, and I'm still not entirely convinced Franny McNeer's death is connected to the other four. And, as yet, we know almost nothing about either the Bernice Carr case or the Holly Wilson case."

"We should be able to get a copy of what they have on Holly Wilson," she replied. "Detective Harper is nice, and she was more than cooperative."

"That was because Tiffany Delgado is a cold case. Holly Willson is not. In fact, it's not even a day old yet. I reckon they'll throw us out. I know I would."

"You're so negative sometimes, Tucker," she said, smiling at him. "You're a real glass is half empty kind of guy. Try to be positive, see the bright side of things."

"I'll happily look at the bright side," he said as he turned off the interstate. "Why don't you give me something?"

She thought for a minute but then shrugged.

"Hah, gotcha," he said. "You can't think of anything, can you? And no, missy, I can't think of anything either. We're in over our heads, and I don't like it. And how about this: suppose Franny's death isn't connected, and Luthor *did* kill his wife? Have you thought about that? What are you going to say to Vinnie?"

Mallory heaved a sigh and pursed her lips, not wanting to admit it was a scenario she'd thought of herself several times, always pushing the thought out of her mind.

"I... I... think... Oh dear, Tucker. I don't know. I just..." She trailed off, speechless.

"Hey," he said. "It's okay. There will always be times like this. Times when we don't even know which way is up. But we'll get through them, as we'll get through this one." *Don't lie to her, Tucker,* he thought, as something deep at the back of his mind dragged him back to the Marsha Cline case. *I really screwed that one up.*

"Okay," he said, "here we are. There seems to be a lot of activity. Let's get to it."

They went inside where, much to Mallory's relief, they found Marcy at the reception desk.

"Miss Carver. Nice to see you again. You'll be wanting to see Finn, I presume?"

"Please," Mallory said, nodding.

"Well, let me see what I can do. She's kinda busy, but she can always say no, can't she?"

She picked up the phone, made the call, asked the question, listened to the answer, then said, "Yes, ma'am." And she put down the phone, stepped out from around her desk, and said, "You're in luck. Follow me, please. They're waiting for you in the conference room."

The minute they walked into the room, everything changed. The FBI had arrived and taken charge of both the Holly Wilson case and the Tiffany Delgado case, but that wasn't all.

Tucker was just about to turn around and walk right out again when, "Hello, Tucker. I was hoping to see you."

Tucker inwardly sighed and shook his head, then said, "Hello, David."

He said it calmly enough, but inwardly he was panicking. He'd been taken completely by surprise.

"What are you doing here?" he asked.

"Interstate crime is federal jurisdiction, you know that, Tucker," David Lewis said, smiling. "Why don't you introduce me to your... charming partner?"

Tucker looked at Mallory. She appeared to be impressed. He looked again at his onetime partner and said, "David Lewis, Mallory Carver."

"Pleased to meet you," they said together and then laughed.

"And this," Lewis said, nodding to the dour-looking middle-aged man sitting at the far end of the table, "is Agent Diago Garcia of the Chattanooga Field Office. He'll be working with me and, by extension, you as well, I hope." He smiled at Tucker.

"So, I'll ask you again," Tucker said. "Why are *you* here?"

"Why don't you both sit down and I'll tell you?" Lewis said. They did. They sat down at the table, and he paused for a moment, then said, "You asked what I'm doing here. Well, it's for two reasons. The first is, when I saw this come up on the Chattanooga Field Office roster, I thought it might be a good way for us both to mend some fences and perhaps rekindle what was to me a rather precious friendship. No!" He held up a hand. "Please let me finish, Tucker. I know we've had our differences and that you blame me for... Well, this is not the time nor the place to reopen old wounds. Can we set those aside for now and deal with the here and now?"

Tucker nodded slowly, obviously unhappy with the situation. But he had little choice other than to agree or get up and walk out. He chose the former and nodded.

"Good," Lewis said. "In that case, I'll bring in Detective Harper and bring you all up to speed." And he left the room.

David Lewis, six-two, slim with black hair and a long, narrow face, was in his late forties, or maybe even in his early fifties. Tucker had never known just how old his ex-boss and partner was. Most of what he could remember was contained in those final few weeks when David had put him in charge of protecting Marsha Cline, a key witness in a double homicide. Marsha had been only nineteen when she was shot dead, and Tucker had never forgiven himself, or David. He'd quit the FBI a few weeks later and had never looked back, although Marsha still haunted his dreams.

"Don't," Tucker said as Mallory opened her mouth to speak. "I don't want to hear it, and I will *not* work with him. We'll hear what he has to say, and then we'll get out of here."

Lewis returned a moment later with Detective Finn Harper. Mallory introduced her to Tucker, and then Lewis took over the meeting.

"The second reason I'm here," he began. "As I mentioned, I saw the Tiffany Delgado case on the CFO roster. I also saw that someone, as yet unknown, had linked the case to those of Elaine May and Bernice Carr in Tennessee, thus making it FBI jurisdiction. Rather than assign it as I normally would have, and after a little research during which your name came up, I took it upon myself. I arrived here in Ringgold late yesterday. I came here early this morning and was informed there had been a fourth murder, that of Holly Wilson—"

"What about Franny McNeer?" Mallory asked, interrupting him.

"Who?" he asked, frowning.

"Franny McNeer," Mallory repeated. "Greasy Creek, Tennessee. She was murdered in her bed eight years ago. She was stabbed forty-three times. Her husband is doing life in Riverbend. That makes five cases. His brother hired us to find the real killer."

Lewis slowly shook his head while Tucker stared stoically at him.

Lewis shook his head. "No, I didn't know about that one, probably because it was solved. Anyway, as I was—"

"Wait," Mallory said. "You're blowing it off because it was solved? No way. There's an innocent man in prison, and we're going to get him out. Look, Franny was stabbed forty-three times in her bed, no signs of a break-in. Elaine May thirty-seven times. Tiffany Delgado thirty-three times. And you're telling us the McNeer case is not connected?"

"Typical," Tucker muttered just loud enough to be heard by everyone in the room.

Lewis looked sharply at Tucker, then said, "I'm not saying that. What I'm saying is, it's not an open case so—"

"Well, reopen the damn thing, then," Tucker snapped. "The

McNeer case is why we're here. If it's not to be part of the investigation, then we don't need to be here." And he began to rise from his chair.

Mallory put a hand on his arm and said, "Let's hear him out, Tucker."

Tucker paused, glanced at her, nodded, and then settled back down in his chair and stared at Lewis.

"I know how you feel, Tucker. I really do, but we can work together on this. It'll be like old times."

Tucker sat absolutely still, his body rigid, then, "Are you frickin' serious, David? Like old times? Do you think I don't remember *the old times?* I remember them every night when I go to sleep, and in my dreams, and when I wake every morning. You let those two bastards walk free to kill Marsha. I was there. I watched them shoot her in the head. I have this to remember those old times." He held out his hand, palm up, to show the scar. "And where were you? Boozing it up in Cleary's Tavern. You can keep your old times, David. I want no more of it. You want us to work together? Fine. You officially reopen the McNeer case. We'll work together, but we'll keep it purely professional."

Lewis stared at him for a long moment, then picked up the phone, punched in a number, waited for the answer, then said, "I want everything you can find on…" He looked at Mallory.

"Frances McNeer, July 8, 2016."

"A 2016 case. Victim Frances McNeer. Location, Chattanooga, Tennessee."

"Greasy Creek," Mallory corrected him. "Polk County."

"Make that Polk County, Tennessee, and I want it soonest. Got it?" He waited for a moment, then nodded and said, "Then go get it. Have it copied and send a copy to me here. No, wait."

He looked at Mallory and said, "I take it you have a copy?"

"We do, but how complete it is, we're not sure. The source —the sheriff's department—is less than reliable."

He looked at Harper, his eyebrows raised in question. She shook her head.

"Make that three copies," he said into the phone, "and I want everything they have. Go now, and make the copies yourself. If you have problems, call me." And he put the phone down.

"That good enough, Tucker?" he asked.

Tucker nodded, his jaw set, his eyes narrowed almost to slits. He was visibly upset. Mallory had never seen him like this before and she was deeply concerned.

"Very well, then," Lewis said. "Let's get on with what we have. Setting the McNeer case aside until I have the file, what we have is this: Two killings in Tennessee and now two here in Ringgold and maybe a fifth in Tennessee." He smiled at Mallory, ignoring Tucker's icy glare. "I have files for you from the Decatur, Tennessee Sheriff's Office and the Cleveland, Tennessee Police Department, and from Detective Harper here." He glanced at her, then continued, "for the Delgado case. It's too soon for the Holly Wilson case, but I'll tell you what I know."

He paused for a moment while Finn Harper handed out the files, and to gather his thoughts, then said, "Holly Wilson, age thirty-one, was found dead in her bed at six this morning by her twelve-year-old son, Michael. Preliminary reports indicate she was stabbed to death. How many times we won't know until the autopsy. The coroner estimated the time of death to be between eleven last night and one in the morning. That's basically all I have for the moment. You'll note the similarities between the victims and the killer's MO. Any thoughts, anyone?"

"We already have Finn's Delgado file and the one from Cleveland," Mallory said as she leaned forward and put the copies on her desk. "The one we didn't have is the one from Decatur, Bernice Carr. Thank you. Now, you asked for thoughts. Well, I have one. I was here, Finn," Mallory said. "I saw Holly pleading for help with one of your officers. I heard him tell her there was nothing he could do. She claimed she was being stalked. I heard her say she'd complained to your department several times, but no one would listen to her. Did you know about that?"

"No. I didn't," Harper said. "Did you, by any chance, get the name of the officer?"

Mallory shook her head.

"I'll look into it," Harper said.

"Tucker," David said quietly. "I know you and Mallory have done a lot of work on these cases. Do you have anything to share?"

Tucker looked at Mallory and nodded. She reached for her shoulder bag, opened it, retrieved a file containing more than eighty single-spaced printed pages, and handed it to Lewis. "You'll find it's all collated and in chronological order, beginning with Elaine May and ending with Franny McNeer," she said. "It also includes my notes on my interviews and Tucker's, too. I hope you find it all helpful."

Lewis flipped slowly through the pages, then looked at her and said, "This is amazing. It's so… well done. I'll have it copied and returned to you. I need time to go through it, but—"

"Thank you for the kind words, Agent Lewis, but there's no need to return it," Mallory said. "I have it all on my laptop, and I record all my interviews on my phone, even some of those when Tucker and I are discussing... strategy."

"You what?" Tucker said, frowning. "You never told me..."

"It wasn't relevant," she replied. "Everything I recorded was/is work-related, even here." She smiled and held up her phone. "It's always nice to have a complete recording of all business proceedings. That way, there's no argument as to what might, or might not, have been said. Don't you agree, Agent Lewis?"

Lewis looked flabbergasted. Finn Harper, who was seated to Lewis's left, was smiling. She winked at Mallory and nodded, unseen by Lewis, who continued to stare at her.

"What?" she asked innocently.

"Oh... nothing really," he said. "I was just thinking what an enterprising young woman you are. You're very lucky to have her on your team, Tucker."

"She is my team," Tucker snapped. "Can we get on with this, please? We have places to be."

We do? Mallory thought. *That's news to me.*

"I see from this that you've already interviewed several persons of interest," Lewis said, still flipping through the file. "I'll study these, of course, but for now, there's nothing we can do about the Wilson case. Forensics has the crime scene locked down, and it's unlikely we'll have access for at least a couple of days, hopefully sometime on Monday. Nor will we have the autopsy report anytime soon. These rural coroners do like to take their time. No insult intended, Detective Harper."

"None taken," she replied.

"In the meantime, I have a couple of interesting prospects we need to interview: Morris Watson and Levi Rogers. Rogers is Carr's ex-husband, so he's definitely a person of interest.

Watson is something else entirely. He was, apparently, friendly with Carr, *and* he was also one of Elaine May's regular clients. Quite a coincidence, don't you think?"

Neither Mallory nor Tucker answered. They just looked at each other.

"No comment, huh?" he said with a smile. "Okay, so here's what I think we should do. These two are a priority, so how about this: I'll track down Levi Rogers, and you and Mallory take on Morris Watson?"

"I don't—" Tucker began, but before he could finish, Mallory interrupted him.

"We're in," she said, ignoring Tucker's angry look.

"Good," David said. "You have Watson's rap sheet. It's included in the Carr file, as is Levi Rogers. So, that leaves Holly Wilson. There won't be much happening there for a couple of days, so I assume you'll oversee that for now, Detective Harper?"

Harper nodded.

"About the Franny McNeer case," Mallory said.

"Yes?" Lewis replied.

"Are you going to include it as part of the overall investigation?"

"Well, I haven't seen the file yet—"

"But you have to admit the stalker MO fits, right?" Tucker asked.

"Well… yes, but…" He caught the look on Tucker's face, then nodded and said, "Yes, it does, and when I've had time to go through the file, I'll give you my decision. In the meantime, we've all got work to do. I suggest we get on with it."

They all rose slowly to their feet and began to file out of the conference room.

"Tucker, if you'll give me a minute," Lewis said.

Tucker paused at the door, turned, faced him and said, "I know what you're about to say, David, and I don't want to hear it. I told you if you'd reopen the McNeer case, we'd work together, but on a purely professional basis. One, you haven't yet said you'll reopen it. You simply said you haven't yet read the file. And that's typical of you, David. You say one thing and mean another. Second, you're not my friend, and on thinking about it, you never were. You were always out for yourself and your career. So, professional?"

Lewis nodded slowly, maintaining eye contact with Tucker. Then he said, "Professional." And held out his hand.

Tucker ignored it, gave him a grim look, then brushed past him and joined Mallory, who was waiting for him a few yards on down the corridor.

"I heard all that, Tucker. Don't you think you were a little hard on him?"

"No!" Tucker snapped.

"You have to give him a chance—"

"Me? Give *him* a chance?" he snapped, interrupting her. "No. He promised she'd be safe. I told him repeatedly that she was in danger, but would he listen? No. He was too full of himself and his career to listen. Yes, I blame him for it, but I also blame myself, too. If she'd never met me, she'd probably be alive today."

"You can't go on like this, Tucker," Mallory said as they reached the end of the corridor. "This Marsha Cline thing is eating you alive. There was just one of you. There was nothing you could have done."

"And there it is," he snarled. "Just one... Just one agent. Me, to guard a poor kid I'd persuaded against her will to testify. Yes, that was me. If I hadn't... He promised she'd be safe. If he had just... I don't want to talk about it, okay?" He paused, then put a hand on her shoulder, brought her to a standstill, stepped around in front of her, faced her and said, "And don't you ever do that again, tell someone we're in without consulting me first. Understand?"

Mallory was stunned by his intensity. "I'm sorry, Tucker. I didn't mean—"

"I know you didn't," he snapped, "and that's the problem. You don't think. You never do. Look, I appreciate your enthusiasm. It's one of the many things I like about you, but this is my company, small as it is, and every decision we make, even the small ones, has a direct bearing upon whether or not we're successful. We're a team. We make decisions together. We must. If not, it will all come crashing down around our ears. Now, against my better judgment, we'll work with Lewis, but I'm going to watch him like a frickin' hawk, and at the first sign of duplicity, we're out; no arguments. Do you understand, Mallory?"

"Yes, I understand," she whispered.

It was already early afternoon when they walked out of the Ringgold Police Department into bright sunshine.

"Look," Tucker said, shading his eyes with a hand. "I've had enough for today. That…" He turned and nodded at the glass doors behind them and then continued, "was a shock I wasn't prepared for. I thought I'd seen the last of David Lewis, and to walk in there and be confronted like that… Well, I need to do some thinking. So, I suggest you go home and take the rest of the weekend off. I'll take you back to your car."

Mallory nodded. She could tell he was in no mood to talk, so they made the trip in almost total silence.

It was almost one-thirty when they arrived back at the office, and the first thing Mallory did was grab the Carr file and make a copy. Then she went into the house, where she found Tucker seated at the kitchen table.

She stood for a moment at the open door, then said, "I just wanted to tell you I'm sorry. Please forgive me."

Tucker looked up at her, stared at her for a moment, then stood, walked up to her, put his hands on her shoulders and kissed her gently on her lips; then he said, "There's nothing to be sorry for, and nothing to forgive. Now go get Annie and go home. I'll see you here first thing on Monday morning. Stop by Hardee's and get us something to eat."

"But—" she began, totally stunned by what had just happened.

"No buts," he said, smiling at her. "Go home."

She stood for a moment staring at him, not knowing what to say. She bit her bottom lip, then nodded and turned slowly away.

She didn't remember the drive to the doggy day care, nor the ride from there home. She was in a state of disbelief mixed with euphoria. Half of her couldn't believe he'd kissed her, the other with a stunned sense of what it might mean.

It was on the lips, she thought. *Not the cheek... or the forehead. On the lips. Oh, my gosh. What just happened? Monday morning? I can't wait till then, can I? Oh gosh. Oh, my. Frickin' hell. What's the matter with me? It was just a peck. It meant nothing... didn't it?*

Back at the office, at just after five, and with a stomach full of pizza and beer, Tucker settled himself down on the couch in his living room and opened the Carr file. Then he leaned back, clasped his hands together behind his neck, closed his eyes and smiled, remembering the stunned look on Mallory's face when he kissed her. He also remembered how soft her lips had felt on his and how sweet they'd tasted. But then he wondered, *What the hell did I do that for? I shouldn't have done it. It wasn't fair to her. She works for me, for Pete's sake. What the hell was I thinking? Hmm, she didn't seem to mind though, did she?* He made a face. *She didn't say she liked it, either. You didn't give her a chance to, you stupid ass. Maybe I'd better call her... apologize. Hmm. Not tonight. Tomorrow, maybe. Geez, I wish...*

He opened his eyes, heaved a sigh, leaned forward, and took Morris Watson's rap sheet from the file.

Geez, that's one hell of a rap sheet, he thought.

Watson was forty-four years old. Of those forty-four years, he spent twelve of them in prison: five separate sentences ranging from six months to four years, all but one of them for burglary. The exception was the one for beating up a working girl. He'd gotten six months for that, and he'd been arrested but never charged three more times for similar events.

And this guy has a thing for prostitutes. May was a hooker. Carr wasn't. Why was he questioned in the Carr case, then? I guess I'll find out...

He yawned widely, closed his eyes again, and his semi-conscious mind was soon filled with images of Mallory Carver.

He woke three hours later at eight-thirty-five, startled. By what, he didn't know. He looked around the silent room. The curtains were open, and it was dark outside. He picked up his phone. He'd put it in silent mode. He checked for messages. There were none. He checked for missed calls. There were none. He set the phone down, disappointed.

Huh! he thought. *I guess I must have been overthinking it.* He stared at the phone for a moment, then shook his head and went upstairs, took a shower, poured himself a drink, then turned on the TV and tried to relax. He watched a movie: *Mission Impossible Ghost Protocol. Really?* he thought, unimpressed by the unrealities of it all in general and Tom Cruise in particular. *They say he does all his own stunts,* he thought. *Hard to believe, but if he does, way to go, Tom.*

He turned off the TV at a little after eleven-thirty that evening and went to bed, but sleep didn't come easily. He tossed and turned for most of the night with visions of masked men stabbing, stabbing... stabbing...

At almost the same time as Tucker opened his file, Mallory, a little more than seven miles away, on the couch in her living room, after a meal of leftover spaghetti and the remains of the bottle of Pino Grigio, opened her copy and extracted the Watson rap sheet, and after she'd scanned through it, she had a similar reaction to Tucker. *Why did they question him about Bernice Carr?*

She put the rap sheet down and began to read through the file. More than two hours later, she was almost three-quarters of the way through it when she came across the reason. Watson, so it seemed, was a long-time friend of Bernice Carr. *Ah, they were in high school together,* she thought. Then, as she read on, she frowned. There was a credit card receipt for an oil change at the service station where he worked. It was dated just two weeks before her death. It was a tenuous connection, but a connection, nevertheless.

That's weird, she thought. *Coincidence? We don't like those, do we, Tucker... Tucker... He kissed me. I wonder...* She looked at her phone, then at her watch. It was eight-thirty. She shook her head and went back to reading and thinking.

So, it looks like Watson knew May and Carr. Hmm, I wonder if he knew Franny, or Tiffany... or Holly. Oh gosh, maybe that's the link, the service station.

She flipped through the other three files but could find nothing to indicate that might be the case. Then she heaved a sigh and relaxed, sucked on her bottom lip, shook her head.*Franny lived less than an hour away from the mall, but that's irrelevant since the mall is the only really decent shopping center anywhere near. Tiffany lived just down the road from the mall, and so did Holly. Elaine lived in Cleveland, fifteen minutes from the mall. And Bernice was also less than an hour away, but it's a straight arrow down Highway 58. Hmm... all roads lead to Hamilton Place Mall, so it seems. I wonder if that's the connection. Could the killer be working there, I wonder? Whew, if he is, and it has to be a he, right? If he is, it's going to take a lot of interviewing to find him.*

Finally, she went to bed, too, but, unlike Tucker, she went to sleep almost immediately, a slight smile on her lips.

18

MONDAY MORNING, DECEMBER 9

Sunday passed quietly. Tucker didn't call, much to Mallory's disappointment. She was tempted, not for the first time, to call him but couldn't think of a good reason why she should, so she didn't. She took Annie for a long walk in the morning, called Jen, her sister, and talked to her for almost an hour, went to the store and stocked up on frozen dinners. Then, after eating a spaghetti dinner, sat down on the couch and stared at the mess of open files and scattered papers.

It took her almost thirty minutes to tidy them up. By the time she had, she was thoroughly fed up and wanted little more than to simply relax with a good book, a glass of nice wine, and the box of Lindor Truffles upon which she'd splurged while at the store.

By six that evening, the truffles were gone and so was two-thirds of the bottle of Pino Grigio.

Mallory woke early the following morning, Monday,

excited at the thought they were going to be talking to Morris
Watson.

She showered, blow-dried her hair, dressed in jeans and a
white roll-neck sweater, fed Annie, ate some cornflakes with
two-percent milk, still feeling a little guilty at the way she'd
demolished the chocolates the day before, then loaded Annie
into the car and dropped her off at her sister's.

Jen was in a funny mood and wanted to talk, but Mallory,
wanting to get to the office, cut her off, promising to spend
some time with her that afternoon. And then she drove to
Tucker's office, excited at the prospect of seeing him and
hoping he'd be in a better mood than when she left him.

It was eight-thirty when she arrived at the office, a bag of
Hardee's sausage and egg biscuits in hand. She unlocked the
door and let herself in to find the office empty: no Tucker.

She frowned. It wasn't like him not to be there. He was
always there early. She looked at his desk—it was neat and
tidy—then at hers: it was just as she'd left it. She looked at the
adjoining door. It was closed. Also unusual.

Hmm, I wonder if he's okay? she thought as she walked to the
door, opened it and stepped through into the house.

Geez! she thought as she stared around the living room.
What the hell?

The place was a shambles and, at first, she wondered if
there'd been a break-in, but soon realized there hadn't. There
were files and photographs scattered across the coffee table,
more on the floor, along with assorted papers and reports.
And, in the midst of it all, lying on the couch, wearing only a
T-shirt and boxers, was Tucker, fast asleep, breathing deeply.

Wow! she thought as she looked at her watch. *I need to get
him moving.*

She went to the kitchen, set the coffee maker brewing,

waited until it finished, then poured a huge mug of coffee and took it into the living room to find Tucker sitting up rubbing his eyes.

"Wow," he said. "Sorry. I fell asleep last night."

"That's obvious," she replied. "Here, drink this." She handed him the coffee.

"Thanks." He took it from her, sipped, closed his eyes, sipped again, then set the cup down among the detritus on the coffee table and said, "Give me a few minutes to go take a shower and get dressed. Sorry. I must look... Oh, never mind." He tilted his head toward the door. She got the message and left him to it.

It took him more than a minute, but by nine-fifteen he'd joined Mallory in the office, dressed in jeans, a white fisherman's sweater, and carrying a heavy leather, sheepskin-lined bomber jacket in one hand and a mug of coffee in the other.

"Okay," he said brightly after setting the coffee on his desk and hanging the jacket on a hook on the office door. "What's the plan? I'm thinking we go find Morris Watson. He has some explaining to do. And I think there might be some kind of connection to the mall. But first... Breakfast. And, speaking of the mall, there's a nice place in the food court. What d'you think?"

"But I brought Hardee's," she protested.

"You did, and I put it in the fridge. I want something more... substantial and... I want to take a quick look around, with different eyes than just a shopper."

"Okay, you're the boss," she said and rolled her eyes. "Lead on, Macduff."

He nodded, drained what was left of his coffee, set the mug back down on his desk, took his holster and Glock 17 from the desk drawer, and clipped the rig to his belt.

"You think you're going to need that?" Mallory asked.

"You never know," he replied, smiling. "How about you?"

She smiled at him and patted her shoulder bag.

"Before we go," he said. "About Saturday—"

"Yes, about Saturday," she said, interrupting him. "My turn." And she stepped forward, kissed him lightly on the lips, and said, "Ready?"

He looked at her for a second, then smiled, reached out and pulled her to him, and kissed her properly.

"Now I am," he said as he turned her loose.

"Oh, my God," she said as she stared at him. "Are you serious?"

"As a heart attack," he replied, grinning. "I've been wanting to do that for a very long time. Shall we go?"

"Yeah… Yeah… You did take your damn time. But wow. Tucker?"

"Yes, I know. Me, too. We need to talk, but not now. We have work to do."

Mallory, still stunned by what had happened, watched as he donned the bomber jacket, then followed him out to his car, her mind whirling. This was a game changer, in more ways than one. He was right; they needed to talk, and soon.

"I meant to come over to see you yesterday," he said as she pulled her door shut and clicked the seatbelt. "But… well… You know."

"I almost called you," she said quietly. "Several times."

He looked sideways at her, smiled, then reached out, took her hand and squeezed it.

Mallory was… Her heart was thumping. Her mouth was dry, and she was, for once, speechless.

Tucker found a parking spot near the front entrance. "I'm

thinking The Big Yellow Egg," he said as they walked together into the mall. "That good for you?"

"Umm, err, yes, of course," she replied.

They found a table and sat down to wait, Mallory nervously fiddling with the hem of her sweater.

"Look," he said. "Just relax. Everything will be fine. We'll sort it out later, okay? Now, just take a deep breath and relax. Get your head together. We have work to do."

She nodded and did as he suggested, took a breath and watched the waitress approaching.

"Tell me about David," she said, desperate to change the subject. "I think it's great that we're working together. You know, with the FBI."

"No," Tucker replied sharply. "No, it's not good, and I don't want to talk about Lewis. Besides, there's nothing to tell, other than he was my boss."

"That's not true, is it? You blame him for what happened to that teenager, don't you? What was her name, Marsha... something?"

"Cline. Marsha Cline. She was eighteen, and no; the blame was mine."

"How could you be to blame for what happened? I don't believe it."

"Well, you would be wrong. She was a witness to two murders. She didn't want to testify, but I persuaded her. I also promised her we'd keep her safe. We didn't, and she died. Case closed. Now can we talk about something else, the case in hand, perhaps?"

She looked at him. His face was pale, and he was obviously upset. She reached out and put her hand on his. He withdrew it, as if her hand was red hot. She leaned back in her chair, bewildered.

"Sorry, I didn't mean..." he began, realizing he'd hurt her feelings, then trailed off.

It was at that moment the waitress arrived at their table and introduced herself.

"Good morning. My name's Jessie. What can I get you to drink?"

"Coffee for me, please," Mallory said and looked at Tucker. He merely nodded.

"I'll be back in a minute with your coffee and to take your order," she said with a smile and turned away.

Tucker watched her go, frowning slightly.

"Hey," Mallory said. "Eyes off. I'm over here."

He looked at her for a moment, then said, "There's something about that girl... I can't put my finger on it, but she... reminds me of someone."

He shook it off, then said, "Look, Mallory. About what happened back there. I don't think it's a good—"

"Stop," she said, cutting him off. "I know where you're going. We can't do this here. Let's have a nice breakfast and then maybe this afternoon, after we've both had time to think about it, we can talk about it, over dinner, perhaps."

He nodded reluctantly but said nothing.

The waitress brought their coffee, and they ordered. Tucker noticed her name tag proclaimed her to be Jessie Mills, and he made a mental note of it.

19

They arrived at the Pitt Stop Service Station on Gunbarrel Road at a few minutes before ten thirty to find it busy with both bays filled and four more customers in the waiting room.

Tucker looked around for the guy named Pete, but there was no sign of him, so he supposed he must be in the shop. Instead, he approached the counter where a young lady was watching them.

"How can I help you?" she asked. "D'you need a full service or just an oil change?"

"Neither," Tucker said. "I'm looking for Morris Watson. Is he here?"

She didn't answer. Instead, she made a face, picked up the phone and broadcast, "Morris Watson to the service desk. Morris Watson to the service desk." Then she put down the phone and said, "He'll be just a minute if you'd like to take a seat."

Morris Watson was, in Tucker's opinion, the epitome of the word creep. He was about five-ten, well-built, tanned, with dark brown hair and two days of stubble. He was wearing jeans and a black T-shirt that was at least one size too small for him. The thin material sharply defined his biceps and pecs, and when he spotted Mallory as he strode confidently into the waiting room, his lips curled into what Tucker described later as a shit-eating grin.

Tucker and Mallory both stood. He approached them and stopped in front of them, just a little too close for Mallory's comfort.

"You looking for me?" he asked, never taking his eyes off Mallory.

"I take it you're Morris Watson?" Tucker asked.

"You got it," he said, still staring at Mallory. "Who are you, and what d'you want?"

"I'm Tucker Randall. I'm a private investigator. This is my associate, Mallory Carver. We'd like to talk to you about Bernice Carr."

"Oh yeah? What about her? Last I heard, she was dead." And still he hadn't taken his eyes off Mallory.

"Hey," Tucker said. "Stop that. You're making her uncomfortable."

He turned his head to look at Tucker. The smile had turned into a sneer. "Is that so?" he asked. "Delicate, is she?" He turned again to Mallory, his eyes narrowed, and said, "I'm not making you feel uncomfortable, am I?"

She shook her head and said, "Look, we just need to talk to—"

"And why should I want to talk to you if I make you feel uncomfortable? How about we meet up later and I buy you a drink, or two, and then maybe—"

"That's enough, Watson," Tucker snapped. "Show the lady a little respect. Now, are you going to talk to us, or would you rather talk to the FBI?" He took out his phone and locked eyes with him.

There was a long pause while the two men glared at each other. Watson was the first to crack.

"Okay, okay," he said, raising his hands in mock submission. "You win. We'll go to the breakroom where it's quiet."

He was right. The breakroom was empty, and they took seats at a small round table. Mallory pulled her seat back and sat down, the table between her and Watson.

"You said the FBI," Watson said. "How come? Why now?"

"They've reopened the investigation," Tucker said. "That's all I can tell you. What was your relationship with Bernice Carr?"

"What the f…" He trailed off, then said, "She was my cousin… Well, second cousin, really. You didn't know that?"

Tucker frowned. So did Mallory.

"No, we didn't know that," Tucker replied. "Were you having an affair with her?"

"Are you for frickin' real?" he snapped. "I might be what you'd call a frickin' redneck, but I don't screw family."

"And Elaine May?" Tucker said, continuing without even a blink. "What about her?"

"What about her?" Watson countered.

"So you knew her, too, then?" Mallory said before Tucker could speak.

Watson looked at her and shrugged. "What of it?"

"She was a prostitute," Mallory said.

"What of it?" Watson replied.

"She's dead," Mallory replied. "Stabbed to death. Thirty-seven times. But you knew that, didn't you, Mr. Watson?"

He grimaced, shrugged his shoulders, and said, "What of it?"

"Well," Mallory said. "First your cousin is stabbed to death, then Elaine May, whom you also knew. You were one of her clients, I believe. That's quite a coincidence, don't you think?"

"You know, lady," he drawled. "I think you're trying to tag me for something I didn't do. But you've gotten your ducks all about face. One, Bernie and me were friends, nothing more, and Lanie, well… Yep, but I was more than a client. Sure, I paid her, but me and her… We… it was special, is what it was. I think she was in love with me. I was totally pissed off when I found out she was dead. I might even have married her. So, yeah. I was a client, but I didn't kill her. Nor did I kill Bernie. And you can't prove I did."

"But you do like to hurt prostitutes, don't you, Morris?" Tucker asked.

"Hahaha," Watson laughed. "Are you serious? That's what they get paid for, some of them."

"So why were you charged with assault—what? How many times? Three, four?"

"Three, and the charges were dropped. They just get… vindictive, I guess. No big deal."

"When did you last see her?" Tucker asked.

"See who?"

"Elaine May."

There was a pause. He hesitated, his eyebrows furrowed, then said, "Shit, it was nine years ago, man. That… Friday evening. She came here. It was my turn to work late. We had coffee together, and I was supposed to meet her when I got off at nine, but by the time we'd cleared up and when I finally got out of here, it was getting on for ten. She never turned up."

Tucker nodded. So did Mallory. She was recording the interview on her phone.

"How about Bernice?" Tucker asked. "When did you last see her?"

Watson blanched. He stared at Tucker, then said, "Look, I know what you're trying to do, and it ain't going to work. I didn't kill them women."

"You didn't answer the question," Tucker persisted, locking eyes with him. He paused, then said. "I get it, Morris. I don't think you did kill them. But here's the thing: the FBI is all over this thing. We're working with them, officially, which is why we're here. Now, what we'd like to do is eliminate you as a suspect. But if you don't cooperate, you'll find yourself talking to Agent David Lewis, and he's a real asshole. I know. I used to work for him. So, what's it to be? Us or him?"

Watson bit his lip. Gone was the bravado, replaced with a look of genuine concern.

"Okay," he said. "I saw her that Friday afternoon. She brought her car in for an oil change."

For a moment Tucker was speechless, then he said, "Here? You saw Bernice Carr here the day she died?"

Watson nodded. "Look, I know how that looks, but it's not what you think. I didn't kill either of them."

"What time did you get off that night?" Tucker asked.

Again, there was a long pause before he said, "I worked late that night, too, so nine, as usual."

"And then where did you go?" Tucker asked.

"Applebee's On Brainerd. I had a couple of beers to wash the shit of this place out of my mouth, and then I went home."

"What time did you leave Applebee's?"

"I dunno. Ten, maybe ten-thirty. I dunno. I told that deputy from Meigs County. I never heard no more from him, so I figured he was done with me."

"How about the night Elaine died?" Tucker asked. "What did you do after work?"

"I told you. I was supposed to meet Elaine, but she wasn't there."

"She wasn't where?"

"Starbucks, up on Hamilton Place Boulevard. She wasn't there. I don't think she ever was. I asked a couple of people. They said they hadn't seen her."

"What did you do then?"

"I called her, but she didn't answer. I thought that was kinda strange, so I went on up to her place in Cleveland. I used to go there a lot, you know? But she wasn't there, and her place was locked up tight and the lights were all off."

"And that would be what time?" Tucker asked.

"I dunno. Eleven-thirty... Eleven-forty-five. I never checked my watch. I was tired, man, so I went on home. That's it. That's all I know."

"Can you think of anyone that she might have upset, that might have wanted to hurt her?" Mallory asked.

He grinned at her, then said, "She was a hooker. So yeah, but who or how many? I don't know."

She nodded. "How about friends here?" she asked. "Did Elaine have any in particular?"

He frowned, then said, "Here? You mean here?"

"Yes, I mean here, at the Pitt Stop," she replied.

"None that I know of. She talked to just about everybody, especially the guys, you know? I mean, she was just over-friendly with them all. She was a hooker, right? Why wouldn't she? It's nothing to be ashamed of."

"Anyone in particular?" Mallory persisted.

"I dunno, Pete in the shop, Charlie, who worked the pumps. Me, mostly. I told you. We were close."

"How about Bernice?" Mallory asked.

He pursed his lips and shook his head. "Not that I know of. Just me. Oh, wait, I told that deputy I thought she was cheatin' on that ex-husband of hers. Nasty son of a bitch, he is. Rogers. That's his name. Maybe you should look at him. As I said, I told that deputy, but if he done anything about it, I never heard nothing. Can I go back to work now?"

"In just a minute," Tucker said. "What about Tiffany Delgado?"

"Who?"

"Tiffany Delgado. She was from Ringgold."

He shook his head. "Never heard of her."

"How about Franny McNeer?" Tucker said.

He didn't hesitate. "Never heard of her, either."

"Where were you last Friday night between ten and one in the morning?" Tucker asked.

At that, he grinned and said, "That's an easy one. I was at the Billiard Club on Cherry Street till almost three. You can ask anyone. Why? What's happened?"

Mallory ignored the question and said, "So you must know Ollie Palmer, then?"

"Sure do. He was there, too. You can ask him if I was there. He'll tell you I was."

Tucker nodded, thought for a moment, and then said, "Okay, Morris, you can go, but I wouldn't leave town if I were you."

"Do I need a lawyer?" he asked.

"Do you think you need one?" Tucker responded.

Watson stared at him, shook his head and stood up, then turned away.

"Morris," Mallory called after him.

He stopped, turned and looked at her.

She held up her card and said, "Here, take this. If you think of anything that might help. It has my cell number."

He came back, took the card from her, looked at it, looked at her, smiled slightly, nodded, then turned and walked away without a backward look.

"You think that was wise?" Tucker asked. "Seeing as how he looked at you. He has your number now."

"Maybe, maybe not." She thought for a moment and then looked at him and said, "Well, that was something, wasn't it?" Mallory said. "What do you think?"

"If you're asking if I think he killed those two women," Tucker replied, "I have an open mind. If you're asking me what I think about him, I think he's one slick son of a bitch. He also thinks he's hot stuff. And even though he denies it, I think he has a penchant for beating up on prostitutes. Did you notice how he laughed when I mentioned it, like it was some kind of joke? What do you think?"

Mallory blew out a huge breath, then said, "Well, he has no alibi for Bernice and Elaine, and they were both here the day they died. That can't be a coincidence. Can it?"

"Maybe, maybe not."

"But he does have an alibi for Holly Wilson, and so does Ollie Palmer, by the sound of it. So, if all five murders are connected, that would eliminate both of them, wouldn't it?"

"It would," Tucker replied, "but the Holly Wilson alibi could be bogus, for both of them. And he has no alibi for the May and Carr murders," Tucker said. "And he admits he was there at Elaine's house around the time she died. In fact, I'd bet she was probably lying on the couch while he was outside, if he was outside, not inside. As to Holly Wilson and the others. If we consider there might be more than one killer... That opens up a whole new line of inquiry, and we can eliminate neither Palmer nor Watson. And if they are colluding, and they're providing each other with an alibi..." He trailed off.

Mallory shook her head. "I don't think that's the case. If it was, we'd have known by now, and Watson would have had an alibi for Elaine's time of death, too."

"Look at you," Tucker said, grinning at her. "Aren't you the detective now? Good thinking, Mallory. I'm proud of you—"

His phone rang, interrupting him. He looked at the screen. "It's David. I wonder what he wants."

"..."

20

What David wanted was to meet. They settled on Tucker's office.

David and Agent Garcia were already there when they arrived, and David was obviously in a good mood.

"Hey, you two," he said as he and Garcia exited their black Chevy Tahoe. "We should have gone somewhere for lunch. It's not too late. What do you say, Tucker?"

"I say we stick to the plan," he replied. "I have things I need to do, so here is fine."

David shook his head. "Party pooper," he said. "You never were the life and soul, were you, Tuck? Always the first one in and the last one out of the office. Never the one to go for a beer with the troops." He sighed. "Your call, buddy."

"I thought you wanted to talk," Tucker replied caustically. "A restaurant is not the place. We'll talk here… if we must."

He unlocked the office door and stood aside for Mallory to enter, and then David and Garcia. He stood outside for a moment, gathering his thoughts and breathing the crisp December air.

Asshole! he thought, then took a deep breath and followed them inside to find David already seated behind his desk.

He looked at Mallory. She was seated at her desk, leaving only a single guest chair in front of Tucker's desk. She shrugged and looked away, seemingly unable to meet his eye.

He looked at David.

David grinned at him. "No formalities, huh, buddy? Sit where you like," looking pointedly at the guest chair.

Tucker gave him a wry look and closed the door.

Garcia was standing with his back to the wall next to the door, looking more than a little embarrassed.

"So, how did it go with Watson?" David asked as Tucker stood with his back to the door, leaning against it.

Tucker, thinking he might fetch a chair from the house for Garcia, didn't answer. Instead, he looked at Mallory and nodded.

"Well," she said and cleared her throat. "It went well enough, though we didn't learn much. It turns out that Bernice Carr is Watson's second cousin, and it seems they were friends—"

"Was he having an affair with her?" David asked.

"No. Not from what he said. At least I don't think so. His actual words were, 'I don't screw family.' And I believe him. So does that answer your question?"

David smiled at her. "It does. Please continue, Ms. Carver."

Mallory stared at him, unable to make up her mind if he was taking the mickey out of her or not. She decided not and continued. "So, anyway, we also asked him about Elaine May, and he seemed quite proud that his relationship with her was more than just that of working girl and client. He said they'd been friends." She made quotes with her fingers. "And that he loved her and that he'd even thought of asking her to marry him. Which was, to me at least, a bit of a surprise. He also said he was supposed to meet her the night she died, but she didn't turn up and that he went to her home, but she wasn't there. Tucker thinks she was probably already dead by then. Either that or he killed her." She paused for breath, then continued.

"He's also friendly with Ollie Palmer, claiming they can provide alibis for each other for last Friday night. We haven't checked with Palmer... I mean, what would be the point? If they're buddies, they're going to back each other up, right? Watson was a little short on alibis for the Carr and May murders, though.."

Mallory continued to provide David a narrative of their interview with Watson. In the meantime, Tucker fetched a chair for Garcia and then sat down on the chair in front of his desk, folded his arms, and stared at Lewis.

"So," David said when she'd finished, "that's a lot of information, Mallory..." He made a face, bared his teeth and sucked in a long hissing breath. "We can't rule him out. The alibi for Wilson is iffy at best, and he's a convicted felon. And they could be working together. What d'you think, Mallory? Did he do it? What does your woman's intuition say?"

"If his alibi for Holly Wilson holds up, and if all five cases are connected... No. He couldn't have."

He turned in his chair and looked at Tucker. "Tucker?" he asked, his eyebrows raised in question.

"What Mallory said," Tucker replied. "If the alibi is good, there's no way he could."

"Oh, way to go, Tucker," David said, laughing. Welcome Johnnie Cochran.

Then he was silent for a moment, until, "I still think he's good for it. So he says he has an alibi for last night. But what if he and Palmer are lying for each other? What if they're double-teaming? Maybe they're even working together. Maybe we have two killers."

"Not likely," Tucker said, leaning forward on his chair, his elbows on his knees, his hands clasped together in front of him. "We also talked to Palmer back in November. He has an alibi for both the Delgado and McNeer murders. They might take a bit of checking out, but I think you'll find them to be good, and if so, that would rule him out, too."

"So, we're back to square one," Tucker said caustically. "We have nothing and no suspects."

David nodded. "Basically... yes. I would tend to agree," he replied. "I spoke to Finn Harper while I was on the way over here. The Holly Wilson crime scene was clean, immaculate. She was stabbed either thirty-eight or thirty-nine times. The coroner was unable to specify exactly how many times. And... her throat was cut—that's a first, I think—from left to right. The angle of cut would indicate her assailant was right-handed. There was no DNA present. Not even a stray hair. It would seem, then, that our perp has perfected his craft. I'll have my team research stabbing deaths in the tri-state area over the last twenty-five years and see if we can come up with anything new."

"What about this Charlie guy Watson mentioned?" Mallory asked.

David nodded. "I'll get a warrant for their personnel files. Wouldn't hurt to take a look at all the employees. It's the perfect place to pick up lonely women. Wouldn't you say, Tucker?"

Tucker was about to answer, but Mallory beat him to it. "And how about security footage? There might be some for last night, and I could call them and ask to see the files, too. That might save a little time."

"Hah, good luck with that," David said. "That never works. We'll get nothing from them without a warrant, but by all means, give it a try."

She nodded, picked up her phone and asked Siri to connect her with the Pitt Stop on Gunbarrel. There followed a short conversation, which obviously didn't go the way she hoped, and she hung up.

"We need a warrant," she said ruefully. She was going to say more but was interrupted by a knock on the door.

21

Tucker moved away from the door, turned and opened it and was almost knocked sideways as Vinnie McNeer rushed in.

"What the hell is going on, Mallory?" Then he noticed the two FBI agents. "Oh, sorry," he said. "I didn't know…"

"It's okay, Vinnie," Mallory said. "This is Special Agent David Lewis, FBI, and that's Agent Garcia. They're here to help."

And at that, Lewis almost choked, but he said nothing. Instead, he rose to his feet and offered Vinnie his hand.

"Vinnie McNeer, I presume. Pleased to meet you, sir."

"Why are you here, Vinnie?" Mallory asked.

"I want to know what's going on, is what," he blurted. "It's been three weeks, and I've heard nothing from you. You're keeping me out of the loop. It's almost Christmas and… damn it, Mallory, when are you guys going to get Luthor out of prison? I see this Holly Wilson thing all over the news, so he couldn't have killed her, could he? And you know he didn't kill Franny, so what's the holdup?"

Tucker frowned, looked at his watch. It was twelve-thirty-five. He stepped over to the TV and turned it to Channel 7 and, sure enough, "—it appears Ms. Wilson was being stalked and had asked the Ringgold police for help several times," the anchor was saying. "Wilson was found in her home stabbed more than thirty-eight times. The time of death was established to be between—"

"Where the hell did they get all that?" David snapped.

"—appears to be the fourth death in a series of what the authorities are now calling serial killings. The previous deaths include Elaine May of Cleveland, who was found stabbed to death in her home in July 2015, Bernice Carr of Decatur, also stabbed to death, in April 2016, and Tiffany Delgado of Ringgold in August 2019. She, too, was stabbed to death. In each case, the local police admit they have no suspects, and this reporter learned this morning that the FBI has sent a team led by Special Agent David—"

"Are you frickin' serious?" David yelled. "Tucker, Mallory, is this your doing?"

Tucker shook his head, a grim smile on his lips. "I'd say you have a leak, Davis—"

"Never mind that," Vinnie yelled. "They left Franny out. What the hell?"

"Whoa! Stop!" Mallory shouted, rising to her feet. "Calm down, everyone. This yelling at each other is getting us nowhere. I assure you, Agent Lewis, that neither Tucker nor myself have spoken to the media. It has to be… I don't know. It could have come from Cleveland, Ringgold, Decatur, or even your people. But it doesn't matter. The damage is done, and we have to work through it."

"What d'you mean, it doesn't matter?" Lewis snapped. "D'you have any idea what effect this will have on the public? You want to put a scare into them, just announce there's a serial killer on the loose. If I get my hands on whoever it was, I'll... I'll..." He was obviously livid. "And," he continued, "now the killer knows that not only local police are involved in the investigation, not to mention Randall and Carver, but also the FBI, something we needed to keep under wraps. If he goes to ground—"

"What about my brother?" Vinnie persisted.

Mallory glared at him and shook her head, but David turned to him and said, "Yes, Mr. McNeer. We're doing everything we can, but we have yet to establish that your brother's wife's murder is conn—"

"Oh yes, we have," Tucker interrupted him. "This... This... agent has yet to be persuaded. But Mallory and I are working on it, and I can assure you that we're doing all we can to get your brother out as soon as possible. Now, what I need you to do is go back to work and leave it to us. I promise we'll keep you in the loop, won't we, *David?*"

David glared at him, then nodded his head.

"Right... Well then... see that you do," Vinnie growled. "Don't make me come after you again, okay?" He looked around the room, hesitated, nodded, then turned and walked out the door.

"Whew," Mallory said. "I don't know about the rest of you, but I could do with a cup of coffee. Anyone else?"

They all did, so she went to make it and returned ten minutes later with four cups on a tray.

They spent the rest of the afternoon trying to put the pieces together and put the obvious leak to the press behind them, though Mallory could tell David was inwardly churning with anger.

Finally, unable to contain himself any longer, he said, "Tucker, Mallory, I need to get this media thing off my chest.

You say you're not responsible for the leak, but I have to get to the bottom of it. You know first-hand how dangerous this kind of thing can be. Do you have any idea who it might have been?"

Tucker shook his head and pursed his lips.

Mallory stared at him for a moment, then said, "I think it's pretty obvious. If it wasn't one of your people, it had to have been someone from Finn Harper's office. No one else knew about the Holly Wilson killing, and that's what they're leading with, and they also know the details, and that could only have come from one of her people."

David stared at her. "That makes sense, but why? Why would she—"

"I'm not saying it was Harper," Mallory insisted, "but one of her people, perhaps."

"Yeah, well, I'm going to get to the bottom of it and when I do—"

"What? What are you going to do, David?" Tucker asked. "Charge them with obstruction? I don't think so. Your big city BS won't work with these people. You might think you're dealing with a bunch of hicks, but they are, for the most part, pretty damn savvy."

Lewis stared at him, breathed out audibly, then nodded, seemed to relax, and said, "Maybe you're right. I'll talk to Harper later and tell her to keep a lid on things. In the meantime..."

It was a little after four when they finally called it a day after beating the dying horse for what seemed to Mallory a lifetime. For some reason she couldn't fathom, she was unable to concentrate and, by the time they finished, the dull buzz of the conversation had all but put her to sleep.

"Okay, that's enough for me," David said, finally, and stood up. "This is getting us nowhere. Come on, Diago. Let's go back to Ringgold and see where Harper and her crew have gotten with it. I'll talk to you tomorrow, Tucker, Mallory. In the meantime, I'll get a warrant for the Pitt Stop."

Tucker nodded while Mallory escorted them to the door.

"Thank goodness they're gone," she said and collapsed into her chair. "I don't know about you, Tucker, but I could do with a drink."

Tucker smiled at her and said, "Me, too. You sit still. I'll go get 'em."

He was gone but a few minutes before returning with a bottle of 2018 Purlieu Cabernet Sauvignon Georges III, Napa, and two glasses.

"I've been saving this for a rainy day," he said, pouring her a generous measure. "Looks like I've picked the right day to open it," he continued as he glanced out the window at the darkening sky and then sat down on the guest chair in front of her.

"Cheers," he said as he raised his glass.

"This looks really expensive," she said, glancing at the bottle and then holding the glass up to the light.

"Eh, it's only money," he said dismissively.

"Oh, come on, Tucker..." and then took a sip. "Mmm." She wrinkled her brow. "This is... lovely."

He smiled. "I bought it for you. Look, I'm sorry about David. He hasn't changed. He's a total ass. Always was, always will be."

"You bought it for me?" she asked, frowning.

"Yeah, a couple of... No, more than that. I bought it two weeks after you came to work with me. I had a feeling it would work out, and I thought it would be nice to... I dunno, celebrate, I suppose."

He paused for a second, staring down into his glass, then looked up at her and said, "Look, Mallory. This thing between us—"

"Tucker, stop," she said, interrupting him. "It is what it is, though what it is, I don't know yet. Instead of trying to figure it out, why don't we just go with the flow and see where it goes?"

He put his elbows on his knees, held his glass in both hands, looked up at her and said, "But what if—"

Again, she interrupted him. "But what if what? We're not exactly kids anymore, are we, Tucker?"

And she got up from behind her desk, grabbed the other guest chair, set it down in front of him, sat down, and then, glass in hand, leaned forward, put the tips of her fingers to his cheek and whispered, "My turn," and then she kissed him.

22

Tucker reluctantly put a hand on her arm, gently extracted himself, leaned back in his chair and stared at her.

She smiled at him, sat upright, and said, "Well, aren't you going to say anything?"

And, for once in his life, Tucker was speechless. His mind was in a turmoil. The situation was rapidly escalating out of his control, and he was feeling helpless. *This isn't going to work,* he thought. *Work relationships never do, and I don't want to lose her.*

"Mallory—" he began, then cut himself off, bit his bottom lip, then slowly shook his head. "It won't work. We have to stop this now, before it gets out of hand."

"But—"

"No! No buts. We're partners. We're working together. That kind of thing never works. We'll end up hating each other. Trapped."

"That's ridiculous," she said, reaching for his hand, but he pulled it away.

"Really?" she asked. "Really? Okay. If that's the way you

feel, I'll just quit, because if what you say is true, it won't work either way. You say we'll end up hating each other. I say we'll hate each other if we don't at least try. I can go back to work for Vinnie. That way there will be no working relationship or... Maybe I could go to work for that Starke guy."

He sighed, shook his head, and stared at her for a long moment during which she simply sat still, glass in one hand, the other in her lap, and smiled at him.

"Cat got your tongue?" she asked finally.

"Are you sure you want to..." he began, then stopped, shook his head, and continued, "Of course you are. When were you ever not?"

"What about you?" she asked. "What do you want?"

"I... I... I—"

The office phone rang. He jumped up, went to his desk and picked up the receiver. "Randall and Carver." *Geez, saved by the bell, literally!*

"My name is Jessie Mills. Is this Mr. Randall?"

"It is. How can I help you?"

"I work at The Big Yellow Egg. I served you this morning. And I saw you on TV at lunchtime today." She sounded anxious. Or was it something else?

Tucker frowned. "I wasn't on TV—"

"No, I didn't mean I saw you," she said, cutting him off. "I saw the reporter. She mentioned your name and that you are involved in the serial killer investigation."

Are you frickin' serious? How the hell did they know? He looked at Mallory, who was watching him quizzically.

"Hold on a minute, Ms. Mills, while I put you on speaker... Okay, are you still there?"

"Yes," she replied.

"So, how can I help you?"

"I need to talk to you."

Tucker furrowed his brow and shrugged at Mallory.

"Well…" he began. "We're listening."

"No, I mean in person. I think I'm being stalked. Can I come to your office?"

"She sounds upset," he said with his hand over the receiver. Mallory nodded. "Tell her to come to the office."

He removed his hand and said, "Sure, come on over. We'll be here till five-thirty."

"Thank you, Mr. Randall. I'll be there in fifteen minutes. I have the address." And she hung up.

He looked at Mallory. She had a sly smile on her lips, and it made him feel uncomfortable.

"So, what d'you think that was about?" he asked for wanting something to say.

"I would have thought that obvious, Mr. Detective," Mallory replied. "She said she was being stalked."

"Yeah, that," he said as he sat down behind his desk.

"So, you still haven't answered my question," she said. "So, I'll ask you again. What do you want?"

He stared at her for a long moment, then said quietly, "I want what's best for you, Mallory."

"Good answer, Sherlock," she replied dryly. "So, how do you want to proceed?"

"Slowly," he said.

"Have you *ever* been in love, Tucker?"

"No, not that I can recall… Well, that's not exactly true. There was this girl in second grade, Lucy Walker, her name was. I used to follow her around like a lost puppy. Pretty little thing, she was—Hey!" he yelled as he dodged the whiteboard eraser she threw at him. "Okay, we have to stop this. We have work to do. Mills will be here in a minute. There's something about her... I noticed it this morning. Something familiar. I can't quite put my finger on it."

"I thought so, too," Mallory said, "and I think I know what it is." She stood up and stepped over to the whiteboard. "Look at these," she said, pointing at four photographs. "Elaine, Bernice, Franny, and Tiffany. They all look alike. And, if I remember her correctly, this Mills woman fits the pattern, too. Same hair, same build, roughly the same age."

Tucker was nodding slowly when there was a knock on the door. It opened, and she stepped inside.

"I'm not too late, I hope," she said.

"No, not at all," Mallory said. "Please, come on in and sit down."

Jessie Mills closed the door and took the seat in front of Tucker's desk.

Mallory, still at the whiteboard, looked at Tucker over Mills' shoulder, pointed again at the four photographs, and nodded. She flipped the board over so Mills couldn't see it, then she came and sat down in the seat Tucker had not so long ago vacated.

"So, Miss Mills," he said. "You're being stalked. Have you reported it to the police?"

"Well... no," she replied. "I didn't really think about it until I saw the news this morning, and then I thought..." She shivered visibly, then licked her lips and continued. "It's just a feeling, really. I've never seen him. It kind of began... one day last week. Tuesday, it was. I was at Hamilton Place Mall, you know? And I had this feeling that someone was watching me. It only lasted a minute. Then, the next day, when I got off shift, a car... well, I think it was a car... the headlights followed me home. And then, yesterday, I was in the front yard, cutting back the hydrangeas, when I had this weird feeling someone was watching me. I looked around and there was this black SUV, a RAV4, I think it was, with tinted windows, parked across the street. It drove away when I turned to look at it."

"Did you get the number?" Mallory asked.

She shook her head. "No, I didn't think. I was so taken aback, you know?"

They both nodded. Tucker glanced at Mallory. She was staring at Mills.

"And that's it?" Tucker asked. "You didn't see the driver, and you didn't see anyone following you at the mall?"

"No," she looked down at her hands. "It's just a feeling, really, but seeing as there's this serial killer out there, I thought... I thought I'd better say something, and then, well, when I saw the news, and they mentioned you guys, I remembered I'd waited on you this morning and I thought..." She obviously didn't know what else to say.

"Okay, Miss Mills," Tucker said. "Here's what I want you to do. I want you to go straight from here to the police department on Amnicola Highway and file a report that you think you're being stalked. They will be skeptical, but that's okay. File it anyway and try to be as specific as possible. Then... Look, I don't want to frighten you, but I do want you to take some basic precautions. I want you to keep all of your doors securely locked at all times. Can you lock your bedroom door?"

"No, there's no lock."

"Upstairs or downstairs?"

"Upstairs."

"Okay, when you go to bed, put a chair under the door-knob. Better yet, go to Lowe's and ask for a portable door security bar or have them cut you a piece of two-by-six exactly thirty-six inches long—that will be a lot cheaper and just as good—and jam it under your bedroom doorknob. And keep your phone charged and by your bed. Look, I don't really think you're being stalked. I think what's happening here is possibly autosuggestion. You heard the news, and you got to thinking and one thing led to another, and here we are. Having said that, there's no sense in not taking precautions. Now, have you got all that?"

"I think so," she replied nervously.

"Good," Tucker said. "Now tell me what you're going to do."

"I'm going to report it to the police, and I'm going to Lowe's and ask for a portable door security bar or have them cut me a piece of two-by-six thirty-six inches long."

"And you're going to keep your wits about you. You're not going to talk to strangers. And you must not go anywhere on your own."

"I've got it," she said. "But…"

"Yes, you can call me or Ms. Carver anytime. Here are our cards. Put the numbers in your phone, and if anything untoward happens, call us. Immediately. You hear?"

"Yes. I heard you. Thank you both," she said and stood up. "I feel a lot better now." She smiled and went to the door, opened it, then turned and smiled one last time before closing it behind her.

"So, what do you think?" Tucker asked.

"I think she's scared," Mallory replied, staring at the door, "and rightly so."

"I know she's scared," Tucker replied, "but do you believe her? Do you believe she's being stalked?"

Mallory shrugged, then said, "I think *she* believes she is, but do I believe she is? I don't know. If I knew her better…

But she seems like a strong woman. Not one for hysteria. What about you?"

"I don't know either," he said, then sighed and continued. "I think maybe she heard all that BS on the news and convinced herself she's next. Who the hell could have leaked it?" It was a rhetorical question that neither of them could answer.

"Hey," he said, looking at her guardedly, "would you like to go somewhere nice for dinner?"

"Why, Tucker Randall, are you asking me out on a date?"

"You want to go or not?" he blurted.

"Yes, that would be nice, but it's almost five-thirty and I have to pick up Annie. Then I have to go home and change. You want to pick me up, say about seven-thirty?"

23

Mallory arrived at the doggy daycare at a little after five-thirty to find Annie had had a bath and her toenails clipped. She was also in one of her playful moods, bouncing around on the end of her leash while Mallory paid her bill and chatted with the lady owner, who was enthusiastically yakking on about what a wonderful dog she was.

"I bet you say that about all the dogs," Mallory said, smiling as she handed over her credit card.

"No, no. Not at all. She really is. She is very obedient, smart, and she gets along with the other dogs really well."

But Mallory already knew all that. "It's because she's a Border Collie," she said as she signed the receipt. "We're good for the rest of the week, then?" she asked as she handed her the signed copy.

"Yes, of course. See you tomorrow, then, around eight-thirty?"

Mallory nodded, thanked her, and Annie led her to the car, straining at the leash.

It was almost six o'clock and dark when she pulled into her driveway and parked. She opened the car door, unclipped Annie and leaned back as the dog scrambled over her, out and down onto the concrete, ran a couple of yards toward the front porch, and stopped dead, the fur on the back of her neck and rump raised. She went into point mode, staring at the porch, growling softly.

"Annie, what's wrong?" Mallory, still in the car, reached for her purse, took out the P938 and slid cautiously out onto the driveway.

"Go find it, girl," she whispered, then flipped off the safety as she stepped slowly forward, the gun held at arm's length in both hands, as Tucker had taught her.

Annie trotted to the porch, her nose to the ground, up the three steps onto the porch and there she stopped, hackles raised, growling, pointing at a paper fast food sack from McDonald's.

"Annie, come, heel," she snapped.

The dog turned and leaped down the steps in two bounds and sat at her heel.

"We need to take a look around the back," she said, and, together, they made a circuit of the house, ending back in front of the steps.

Mallory looked at the paper sack, took a deep breath, climbed the three steps, peered cautiously inside using the barrel of the gun to open it, and found a Big Mac and fries.

She bit her bottom lip, frowned, stood up and looked around, back toward the road in time to see a pair of headlights come on and a black SUV drive slowly by and disappear into the night.

She set the safety on the P938, went back to the car, got her purse, slipped the gun inside and went to the house and unlocked the front door. And there she had a second thought. She took the gun from her purse, flipped off the safety and went inside. A quick but breathless tour of her home revealed nothing more. She sat down at the kitchen table, put the gun down on the tabletop, ran her fingers through her hair, then put her elbows on the table and her head in her hands, and there she sat for several moments, thoroughly unnerved, trying to compose herself. Finally, she got up, went to the front door, grabbed the paper sack and then went back to the kitchen and threw it in the trash.

"That was quite a fright, Annie," she said.

The dog sat still, looking up at her, panting softly, her tongue hanging out the side of her mouth.

"I bet you need to go out, right?"

Annie jumped to her feet and ran to the back door.

Fifteen minutes later, with Annie safely back inside eating a full bowl of her special homemade food and all the doors and windows securely locked, Mallory was in the shower, the hot water washing away the rigors of the day, especially those of the last half-hour.

She toweled herself off, blow-dried her hair and then went to her bedroom, wondering what she was going to wear. Not that she had a lot of choice. Ten dithering minutes later, after trying to decide on red or black, she slipped into the little black dress and stood in front of the mirror, barely recognizing herself. The dress was sleeveless, cut two inches above the knee and contrasted nicely with her blonde hair. She nodded to herself, slipped on her taupe sandals with three-inch heels, boosting her height to a little over six-one, then went again to the mirror and stood there for several moments, wondering if it was a little too much. Finally, she sighed, gave it up and decided it would have to do; it was seven-twenty. *Almost time,* she thought as she added a little light makeup to her eyes, cheeks and lips.

Tucker arrived punctually at seven-thirty and rang the doorbell.

"Hey," she said as she opened the door and stood aside for him to enter. "Right on time."

Then she led him through to the living room, turned and was about to speak, but before she could, Tucker said, "Wow! Who the hell are you?"

She blushed, speechless.

"You look…" He wanted to say beautiful, but the word hung there on the tip of his tongue. So he settled for, "Amazing. I've never seen you look like this before. You don't look… real."

"Oh, stop it, Tucker," she said, feeling more than a little pleased with herself. "Would you like a drink before we go? I have some nice scotch."

He shook his head. "Better not. I'm driving, so two drinks only. You ready to go?"

"I am." She turned to Annie, who was on the couch watching their every move, and said, "I won't be long, Annie. You guard the house while I'm gone, okay?" The dog tilted her head and looked quizzically at her, then lay down, put her head between her paws and stared up at her.

"Good girl," Mallory said, then turned to Tucker and said, "Shall we?"

And they did, and Mallory, having decided she didn't want to spoil the evening, said nothing about the paper sack or the car that had been parked just down the street. Was the driver watching her house? Did they put the paper sack on the porch and, if so, why? *I mean, who does that kind of thing?* she wondered as Tucker drove to Ruth's Chris.

"By the way," he said, "David figured out who the Pitt Stop employee is. It's Charlie Gibson. I think we'll go see him tomorrow morning. What d'you think?"

She nodded, then said absently, "Yes, all right." It wasn't until they were seated at their table that he noticed how pale she looked.

"Hey," he said, frowning. "Is everything okay? You look kind of pale."

She smiled at him, reached across the table, took his hand, squeezed it and said, "It is now." *But not really*, she thought, took a deep breath and smiled at him.

They enjoyed a delightful meal together, talked about everything except work and, by the time they were through, she knew more about Tucker than she had in all the time she'd known him. He really opened up to her, about his brother, their family, his upbringing, even his past girlfriends; but simmering at the back of it all, even though he mentioned it only once in passing, was the death of Marsha Cline. And so, two steak dinners and a rather expensive bottle of red wine later, he drove her home.

He parked beside her CRV and walked her to the door. As she was about to unlock the door, he took her arm, turned her to him, then took her in his arms and kissed her.

"Oh...my," she whispered. "Tucker—"

He put two fingers to her lips and said, "I'll see you tomorrow. Sleep well, Mallory."

"Don't you want to come in?" she asked, a little bewildered.

He pursed his lips, shook his head and said, "Yes, of course I do. But not tonight. Lock all your windows and—"

"Yes, I know," she said, cutting him off. "But are you sure you won't come in?"

He nodded, put his hands on her shoulders, and kissed her again. "I'll see you tomorrow," he said, then turned, walked down the steps and back to his car, where he stood and watched until she turned, waved, and then went into the house and closed the door.

24

TUESDAY MORNING DECEMBER 10

Tucker slept little that night. He couldn't get Mallory out of his head, and it perturbed him. He'd experienced nothing like it before, and what he couldn't understand was why now? He'd known her for more than a year. They'd worked closely together all that time, and never once had he felt for her what he was feeling now, but he really wasn't sure *what* he was feeling, and it was that that was keeping him awake.

And so, last time he looked at his bedside clock, it was after two when he finally fell asleep to be awakened by the jangle of his iPhone alarm at six-thirty.

He literally fell out of bed, grabbed the phone, cut the alarm, and then sat with his back against the bedframe, trying to pull himself together.

He made it to the bathroom, took a hot shower, and then turned it cold, almost giving himself a heart attack. He dressed quickly and went downstairs, turned on the local news and ate some breakfast, checking his watch every five or ten minutes.

She finally arrived at a little after eight-thirty to find him sitting behind his desk, nursing a cup of coffee.

"Hey, you," he said as she closed the door. "There's coffee in the pot. Did you have a good night?"

"I did. You?" she replied as she poured herself a cup of coffee.

"Yep," he lied. "There's nothing on the local news about Holly Wilson," he said, more for something to say than anything else.

"No," she replied. "I saw that."

There followed a moment of strained silence before Tucker said, "Have you eaten yet? I haven't, and I thought maybe we could stop by and check on Jessie Mills on our way to the Pitt Stop."

"No, I haven't. Is there anything we need to do here before we go?"

"Can't think of a thing," he replied, his second lie of the morning. There was always plenty to do at the office, but Tucker was always one to put things off until the last minute. "Let's go."

The Big Yellow Egg was busy, as it always was at that time in the morning. Jessie Mills was, as Tucker had hoped, waiting tables and seemed to be in a good mood.

"Good morning," she said, smiling. "My name's Jessie and I'll be your server today," she quipped. "What would you like to drink?"

"I see your sense of humor has returned," Tucker said, looking up at her. "How are you feeling?"

She shrugged. "I'm okay," she replied. "I took your advice. I had Rachel pick me up this morning, and I got one of those door bar thingies. So yeah, I'm okay, I guess."

"Well, that's good," Tucker said. "You know where we are and how to get a hold of us if you need us." Then he looked at Mallory and said, "So, Mallory, what will you have?"

She ordered two eggs scrambled, sausage, grits, toast and coffee, black.

"I'll have the same," Tucker said.

"What's the matter, Mallory?" he asked as Jessie walked away. "You still look… pale."

"Nothing," she replied sharply. For some reason she couldn't define, she was still unwilling to tell him about the paper sack on her porch. "Really. It's nothing. What are we doing for Christmas?" she asked, changing the subject.

That hit him like a bolt out of the blue. Close as it was, he hadn't even thought about Christmas.

"What? Hah, I haven't thought about it," he said.

"Well," she said, "it's just a couple of weeks away, so maybe you should." And that did the trick. Tucker, now sidetracked to something he didn't want to think about, also changed the subject.

He took a sip of his coffee and said, "I wonder if David has a list of Pitt Stop employees. Hold on to your thoughts while I text him." He tapped on his phone for several seconds, then hit send and set his phone down almost at the same moment as their food arrived.

No sooner had they finished eating than his phone chirped, indicating he had an email. He opened the email, read it, then said, "Do you have your iPad with you?"

"Yes. Why?"

"Take it out. It's an email from David with an attachment.

The attachment is too big to read on my phone, so I'm going to forward it to you. I need you to open it so I can read it. It has a list of the Pitt Stop employees, and some of them have records."

"Okay," she replied, taking the iPad from her shoulder bag. "Send it."

She opened the iPad, signed in and, while Tucker tapped on his phone, she went to her email account. Tucker hit send, then looked at her, his eyebrows raised. The email arrived. She opened it, then opened the attachment and handed the tablet to Tucker. All that without saying a word.

Tucker scrolled through the attachment, then looked at Mallory and said, "You want to take notes?"

"How about you talk, and I record it?" she replied.

"Good enough," he said and waited while she set her phone to record.

She nodded, and he began, "There are seven men and eight women on the Pitt Stop staff. We can eliminate the women and concentrate on the men."

Tucker took a sip of coffee and then continued, "First, there's Morris Watson. We talked to him yesterday and decided we can't eliminate him.

"So the rest is as follows. Watson mentioned Charlie Gibson. He's thirty-six. He looks after the pumps and fills in as a sales clerk as needed. He works mostly dayshift. He has a record. He did ten months in County in 2008 when he was twenty for assault. Apparently, he got drunk and tried to rape a female friend. He's been clean ever since.

"Next is Pete Abbott, age thirty-two. Watson also mentioned him. He's a sales clerk, works dayshift seven till seven. No record. I think I met him when I was paying for gas a few days ago.

"Mike Harrell is forty-three. He's a mechanic. Works dayshift seven till seven. No record.

"Larry Talbot, age forty-eight, Mechanic. Dayshift. No record.

"Jarred Marks, age thirty-three. Mechanic. Day shift. Now he has a record. He was arrested in 2015 for bar fighting. The judge let him off with a warning. He was arrested again in 2017 for breaking a man's jaw. He was fined a thousand dollars and given fifty hours of community service for that one. In 2018, he was arrested again. This time for stealing a car. That one got him a hundred hours of community service. He's been clean since. Hmm.

"Finally, we have Jinks Jones, age twenty-five. Mechanic. No record. You get all that?"

She gave him a withering look and said, "Of course I did."

"So," he said, grinning. "What d'you think?"

"I don't know. I've not met any of them yet."

He nodded, caught Jessie's eye, and asked for the check.

He paid the bill, reminded Jessie they were just a phone call away, then looked at Mallory and said, "Let's go meet the cast."

Tucker pulled onto the Pitt Stop lot a few minutes later and parked in front of the convenience store window, taking note of the vehicles in the service bays and the two men working there; one of them was Morris Watson.

Together, they walked through the glass doors into the convenience store and looked around. The register was being tended by an older, frustrated-looking woman.

"Pete around?" Tucker asked.

"Aisle four," she replied without looking at him.

They stepped over to the coolers that lined the far wall and there, at the far end of the store, Tucker spotted the guy he recognized as Pete stocking the shelves.

Pete stood up as they approached, put his hands on his hips and stretched his back.

"Hi," he said. "Looking for more energy drinks? They're back there, to your right."

"Pete Abbott?" Tucker asked.

Abbott frowned, then said, "Yeah. How d'you know my name?"

"I was wondering if we might have a word," Tucker said, smiling at him.

The frown deepened. "What about?"

"My name's Tucker Randall. I'm a private investigator. This is my associate, Ms. Carver. We're looking into the death of Franny McNeer."

"Never heard of her," he replied. "Is this about that serial killer everyone's talking about? I saw something about it on TV this morning. Why would you want to talk to me?"

"Your name came up and—"

"Son of a bitch. It was Watson, wasn't it? I saw you talking to him yesterday. I'll frickin' murder him... Whoa, don't take that the wrong way. I only meant—"

"I know what you meant," Tucker interrupted, smiling at him. "We're talking to everyone who might have known her. You didn't know her, right?"

He shook his head. "Yeah, no. I didn't know her. I never heard of her."

"How about Elaine May?"

Again, he shook his head. "Nope... No, wait. Wasn't she Morris' girlfriend? But that was years ago. She a hooker, wasn't she? I reckon I might have seen her in here, but I don't remember her if I did."

"Tiffany Delgado?"

He shook his head.

"How about Holly Wilson? Did you know her?"

"The blonde on TV? The one that got killed last week? No, of course I didn't," he said, frowning. "Look, what is this? Am I in some kind of trouble?"

"No, of course not," Tucker said. "Where were you last Friday night between ten and one in the morning?"

"Oh, come on, man," he began. "This is ridiculous... I was home. And I was alone." He looked upset, and Tucker didn't blame him.

Tucker nodded, then said, "Thanks for your time, Mr. Abbott. Is Mr. Gibson around?"

"He's out there somewhere, working on pump nine, I think. Hell, I don't know. You're done with me, then?"

Tucker nodded. "Yes, we're done. Thank you again."

"So, what d'you think?" Mallory asked as they walked outside onto the forecourt.

"Oh, he's okay. I told you he's a nice guy."

"You didn't ask him about Bernice," she said as they stood and looked around.

"I didn't think there was any point," he replied. "He didn't remember Elaine, so what were the chances of him remembering Bernice?"

Mallory didn't answer. She looked around and saw Abbott staring at them through the window.

"That must be him," Tucker said, setting off toward a man working on one of the pumps. "You want to take this one?"

"Sure," she said.

Gibson had the front off the pump, exposing its inner workings, and he was on his knees with both his hands inside.

"Mr. Gibson?"

"Yeah," he replied without taking his hands out of the machine.

"Can we have a word?"

"Yeah, but you'll have to give me a minute."

The minute turned into five, but eventually, he pulled out, sat back on his haunches, pulled an oily rag from his pocket and wiped his hands, all the while staring at the inner workings of the pump.

"That should do it," he muttered to himself, then turned his head and looked up at them. When he saw Mallory, he quickly scrambled to his feet, blushing. He offered her his hand, then quickly withdrew it. "Sorry," he said. "Dirty. You want to talk to me? What about?"

"I'm Mallory Carver, and this is Tucker Randall. We're private investigators"—*Well, I will be soon*, she thought—"and we're—"

"I know what you want," he snapped, stuffing the dirty rag into his pocket. "Mo told me all about it after you left yesterday. I don't know nothin' about anything."

"Mo?" she asked, frowning. "Oh, you mean Morris Watson. What did he tell you?"

"He said that you was lookin' into that serial killer thing we saw on TV. Look, lady. I just told you. I don't know nothin' about any of that. So... why don't you just go and leave me alone?"

"It seems some of the victims were known to frequent the Pitt Stop, so we're talking to everyone who worked here over the last ten years, and that includes you, Mr. Gibson. Now, would you rather talk to us or to the FBI?"

He ran his hand through his fair hair, then realized what he'd done, looked at his hand and muttered, "Aw shit!"

He heaved a sigh, shook his head once, then said, "Okay, go ahead. Ask your questions."

"Did you know Holly Wilson?"

"The woman they're talking about on TV? No! Absolutely not."

"Where were you last Friday night between ten and one in the morning?"

"Shit. Here we go," he muttered. "Friday night? I was at the bar in Applebee's on East Brainerd till they closed at eleven and then I went home. I was home by half-after-eleven. That's it."

"Can anyone corroborate that?" she asked.

"Yeah, Mickey. He was working the bar, among other things. Now, are we done?"

"Not quite," she replied. "You say you were home by eleven-thirty. Were you alone?"

"Unfortunately, yes!"

"So you were alone between eleven and one a.m.?" she persisted.

"That's what I said, damn it."

"Do you know Jessie Mills?" she asked.

He frowned. "No. Who is she?"

Mallory shook her head, then said, "Elaine May?"

At that, he grinned and said, "Mo's old girlfriend, the hooker? Sure, I did. Everybody did. I even had me a little of it one time. My, but she was hot, but way too expensive for my blood. What she saw in Mo, I don't know. She could have had her pick. He knew I laid her that one time, and it pissed him off big time. And I know he was pissed at her. Gave her a black eye. What did he say about me? Frickin' rat."

"You say he was angry that you... that you... laid her. How angry?"

Gibson grinned at her. "Angry enough to give her a smack in the eye. He knew better than to mess with me, though. You're asking me if he could have killed her?" He shrugged, still grinning widely, then continued, "Maybe. I dunno. I guess we've all got a little of that in us, given the right circumstances."

"How about you, Mr. Gibson? Did you have it in you to kill Elaine?" Mallory asked.

He was smiling widely now. "I was wondering when you'd get around to that," he said. "No, lady. I didn't kill her. I thought she was pretty damn cool, and I'll remember that night I had with her till I die. Five hundred bucks that cost me, and it was worth every damn dime. She put her heart and soul into her work, that one did, and she was a looker, too."

He paused, stared at Mallory for a second or two, then said, "Look, I know you talked to Morris. He told me you did. He didn't tell me he'd pointed you in my direction, though. I'll have a word with him about that. But let me give you a little advice. Stay on him. He's a nasty little weasel. I think he may even be psychotic enough to have killed those women. I watched him kill a cat once, for nothing, for just being in the service bay. Beat its head in with a wrench, so he did. Wicked little f…" He trailed off, obviously still thinking about the cat.

"So where were you the night Elaine died?" she asked.

"Hah! God only knows. How long ago was it? Seven years? Eight? How the hell should I know?"

"Nine," she said, exasperated.

"So now go ahead and ask about the other dead women," he snarled. "But before you do, I don't know where I was for any of them. Geez, lady. Where were you on… let's say July 10 this year?"

She looked at him, obviously taken aback, then said, "That's not quite the same—"

"See?" he said. "You don't know, do you, and that's only six months ago. So how d'you expect me to remember where I was six years ago? Damn stupid question, if you ask me."

"Well, here's another stupid question for you," she snapped. "You have a record for assault. You were arrested for sexual assault in 2008, and you served ten months. You tried to rape a young woman. What d'you have to say about that, Mr. Gibson?"

He narrowed his eyes and stared at her. "I say that was blown up out of all proportion," he replied. "I was a kid, and I was drunk. Sure, I pushed her a bit too hard. I never intended to rape her. I don't drink anymore, and I've not been in any trouble since."

"But you're on the Tennessee Sex Offenders Register, are you not?"

He took a long, deep breath, then said, "I am. So what?"

"Think about it, Mr. Gibson. Did you know, Bernice Carr?" she asked. "She was a friend of Elaine May."

He shook his head. "No, ma'am. I did not!"

"Tiffany Delgado?"

He grinned at her and shook his head.

"How about Franny McNeer?"

"Nope." He grinned at her, eyed her up and down, obviously liking what he saw.

It was at that point that Mallory's lack of experience became apparent to Tucker.

She hesitated, and Tucker stepped in and said, "All right, Mr. Gibson. Thank you for your time. We may need to talk to you again." He nodded to him and turned away.

"You're welcome," he said, "especially you, lady."

"Pig," Mallory muttered as they went back to the convenience store. "Hold on, Tucker," she said, grabbing his arm. "What was that about back there?"

"Yes, sorry about that. I just got the feeling we were wasting our time," he said, trying to be diplomatic. "He's one tough SOB, but I tend to believe him. He maintained eye contact, and he wasn't bothered by the questions."

"True," she said as they walked toward the service bays. "But he has no alibi for any of them, not even Holly Wilson. And he has all the attributes of a serial killer."

"Hah," he half-laughed. "Yes, I suppose he does. Let's see who else we can find."

"Well, I think he's a good fit," she said petulantly.

Morris Watson met them at the service bay doors, wiping his hands, and said, "What did Charlie have to say for himself, then? I saw you talking to him. Piece of work, he is. Ain't he?" He looked at Mallory and said, "You need to watch him."

"Hello, Morris," Tucker said. "You've had time to think about our chat yesterday. Anything to add?"

Watson grimaced, shook his head, and said, "Can't think of a thing, Detective."

"Who's your friend?" Tucker asked.

Watson turned to look at the young man who'd joined them. He was fair-haired, tall, wiry and obviously worked out.

Watson turned to look at him, then said, "Jinks, say hello to Mr. Randall and... Sorry, ma'am. I forgot your name."

"Carver," she said.

"Mallory Carver," Watson said. "They're what they used to call in the movies, private *dicks*." He emphasized the word dicks.

Jinks nodded but said nothing.

"Jinks Jones?" Tucker asked.

"Yeah, so what?"

"Can we have a word, please? In private?" Tucker asked.

"You can say whatever you want to say in front of him," he said belligerently.

"Beat it, Morris," Tucker said to Watson in a tone that made it clear he would brook no argument.

Watson grinned, nodded, then said, "Careful what you say to them, Jinks. Things have a way of getting twisted, if you get what I mean." Then he turned away and walked to the back of the service bay. There, he sat down on an oil barrel and stared at them.

This kid is too young to have had anything to do with Franny, Carr and May... Tucker thought. *Still, it's worth a shot.*

"Just a few quick questions, Jinks. Can you tell me where you were between ten and one on Friday night?" *Might as well begin there.*

"Yeah, Mo told me about you guys," he said. "I don't have to say nothin' to you."

"That's true," Tucker said, "but if you have nothing to hide, why wouldn't you want to answer our questions?"

Jones shrugged, locked eyes with Tucker, then said, "I was with Jenny, my girlfriend."

"Jenny who?"

"Lawrence. Jenny Lawrence. I was with her at her place all night. You can call her. The number is..."

He gave them the number. Tucker nodded at Mallory. She turned, walked away, and made the call. She was gone only a couple of minutes before returning.

She nodded at Tucker, and he turned and said, "Thank you, Jinks. That's all we need. See? Easy, wasn't it?"

Their next stop was back in the convenience store where they checked on the other employees on the list and found that Harrell was on sick leave, having had hernia surgery on December 3, three days before Holly Wilson's murder. Marks was off until the weekend. And Talbot had the day off.

"If Harrel has just had surgery for a hernia, I doubt he could have been fit enough to have killed Holly Wilson. Hmm, time to get some lunch," Tucker said. "What d'you fancy?"

By then, they were back in the car and she leaned back in her seat and closed her eyes.

"The Acropolis would be nice," she said, her eyes still closed. Then, "Why did you let him off the hook, Tucker?"

"I thought you'd ask that," he replied as he started the engine. "A couple of reasons. One, his alibi checked out, right?"

"It did," she said.

"So he couldn't have killed Holly Wilson and, by extension, neither could he have killed Delgado. As for the others, he would have been in his teens, so I didn't think so. All we needed was a confirmed alibi for Wilson, and we got it. No sense in prolonging an interview when we didn't need to."

"Makes sense, I suppose," she said and yawned.

25

Being a Tuesday lunchtime, Mallory expected the Acropolis to be busy, and it was, though the wait time was only a few minutes.

They were seated by the window at the far side of the dining room opposite one another, something Mallory was—though she couldn't explain why—somehow grateful for.

"Mallory, you've been quiet all morning. Something's wrong," Tucker said, leaning across the table and taking her hand. "What is it?"

She shook her head and squeezed his fingers. "Nothing. Really. I promise."

"Is it… You know?"

"Us, you mean?" she asked, smiling. "No."

"Well, I know you well enough by now to know when something's off. Come on. Tell me."

She locked eyes with him and sighed. "Tucker, it's nothing. I'm probably making a big deal out of it, but—" She cut herself off, shook her head again, then continued, "When I got home last night, I let Annie out of the car, and as soon as she hit the ground she started growling. She knew something was wrong. I followed her to the porch and... and someone had left a bag of McDonald's at the front door. No note. Nothing. Just the bag of food. We checked around the house." She shrugged. "Look, it's probably nothing. Someone being nice. But..." She bit her bottom lip. "Considering what we're dealing with, it's a little unnerving."

He squeezed her hand and was about to speak when the server arrived to take their order. He let go of her hand and leaned back.

The server left, and Mallory said, "Well, any comment?"

"You're probably right," he said. "Much ado about nothing. But... Where's your Sig?"

She reached for her purse, opened it and showed him the weapon nestled in the interior, safety on, hammer cocked.

He nodded. "Keep it with you locked and loaded at all times. Keep your doors and windows securely locked and bar your bedroom door. You need some security cameras. I have some and a spare laptop. I'll come over this evening and install them... If that's okay with you."

"Of course it is. How about I cook spaghetti?"

"That would be nice," he replied, smiling at her as his phone buzzed.

"Hello, David," he said when he answered the phone. "Okay... Uh-huh... Yep... Say..." he looked at his watch, then said, "Two o'clock... Yes... Of course." Then he hung up and shook his head. "He wants an update. Our office at two." Then, under his breath, "Son of a bitch!"

"I heard that," Mallory said. "You have to get over it, Tucker. Put your grievances behind you. Being adversarial is non-productive."

"Easy for you to say," he muttered, then took a deep breath, smiled and said, "I'll try to do better, but only for you."

They arrived back at the office to find David and agent Garcia already there, waiting for them.

"Nice lunch?" David asked as they got out of the car.

"Nice until—"

"Yes, it was very nice, thank you, David," Mallory cut in, giving Tucker the look. He just smiled at her and unlocked the office door, then stood aside for them to enter.

"Coffee, anyone?" she asked brightly.

It was a yes for everyone.

"So," David said. "What have you been up to this morning?"

"Why don't you go first, David?" Tucker said. "How did it go with Levi Rogers yesterday?"

David nodded. "He has a record for violence, as you know, mostly domestic. He's remarried to a girl almost half his age; Alicia Aguirre. She opened the door. Nasty black eye. Said she tripped and fell. I don't believe it. Kid can't be more than twenty-five. I think he's knocking her about."

He thought for a moment, then continued, "His alibi for Friday night is Alicia, which isn't worth a damn. She's scared of him. We asked him about Bernice Carr, his first wife. He said he was out of town on a fishing trip and came home as soon as he heard what happened. Your buddy and his, Morris Watson, called him and gave him the news. So I'm pretty confident it's *not* Levi. As for Delgado; he has a solid alibi for that one. It was easy to confirm. All it took was a phone call.

He was at work, at the Amazon distribution facility on Discovery Drive. Garcia talked to his foreman, and he confirmed it. As to the rest..." He shrugged. "He wasn't working at Amazon before December 2018 when he signed on for the Christmas rush and they kept him on. It's no more than what's in Detective Warner's report. You have a copy, right?"

"We do now," Mallory said. "Thank you."

She handed him and Garcia a mug of coffee, and another to Tucker. Then sat down at her desk with a cup for herself.

"So," David said after taking a sip of coffee. "How did you do?"

"No better than you," Tucker said. "We interviewed the main suspect, Morris Watson. He and Palmer have complementary alibis for the Wilson murder, but they're buddies and would probably back each other up no matter what. And, of course, there's the possibility that they could be working together."

"Maybe we should talk to Palmer again," Mallory said. "About Wilson."

"Yes, I think we should," Tucker said, then to David he said, "We also interviewed a Pete Abbott. He has no alibi for the Wilson murder and was pretty pissed off that Watson had pointed the finger at him.

"We also talked to Charlie Gibson. He did ten months for sexual assault back in 2008, but he's been clean since. He has a partial alibi for the Wilson murder. He admitted he knew Elaine May and that he'd had sex with her, for a fee, but insists he didn't kill her. He can't remember where he was the night she died, but he did point the finger at Watson. He said, and I quote..." He looked at his notes and read, "'He's a nasty little weasel. I think he may even be psychotic enough to have killed those women.'"

"And we talked to Jinks Jones. If his alibi for the Wilson murder checks out, we can eliminate him for that one. And he's too young to have killed May, Carr or McNeer."

"So," David said, "we have some work to do, though it feels like we're at a bit of a dead end. I wonder—"

He was interrupted by the door opening and Jessie Mills bursting into the room, pale as a sheet.

"You've got to help me." She was in a panic, her voice trembling. "Someone's been following me. A car followed me home last night. A black SUV, and I saw it parked across the street from the Egg, just a few minutes ago. It drove away when I went outside and stood looking at it. I tried to get the number, but it was too quick for me. You've got to help me. *Please!*" And she burst into tears.

Mallory got up from her desk, went to her, put an arm around her shoulder, and steered her to her chair.

"Calm down, Jessie," she said gently. "Of course we'll help you. Just... calm down, okay?"

Jessie stopped crying, heaved a shuddering breath, wiped her eyes, sniffled, and nodded.

"We need to see the Egg's security footage," Tucker said. "Mallory and I can do that. Anything more you need from us, David?"

"No, but stay in touch. If there's anything on that footage, let me know ASAP, okay?"

Tucker nodded, and the two FBI agents rose to their feet and left.

"Jessie?" Mallory asked, handing her a tissue. "Would you like some coffee?"

Jessie shook her head and looked ready to burst into tears again.

"Come on, now," Mallory said. "That's enough. You're safe

now. Tucker and I will go talk to your boss and hopefully look at the security footage. What I want you to do is go home. You have a door bar, right?"

"I have three," she muttered. "One each for the downstairs doors, back and front, and one for my bedroom."

"That should do it," Mallory said, taking her arm. "Now then, off you go. We're on it... D'you have a gun?"

Jessie shook her head.

"Hmm, maybe you should."

She looked at Tucker. He shook his head, frowning. "No!" he mouthed, so Jessie couldn't hear him.

"Now look," she said as Jessie rose to her feet. "You have my number, and you have Tucker's. You can call us anytime, okay?"

She watched her go to her car and then closed the door, turned to Tucker and said, "We could have given her a gun. You have plenty."

"Err, no, we couldn't," he replied. "We don't know if she can handle a gun. Hell, Mallory, no one should own a gun, or even handle one unless properly trained. They could be a danger to themselves, much less anyone else."

"Sorry. I didn't think," she replied.

"Let's go take a look at that footage..." he said, then thought for a moment before continuing, "Look, Mallory. I know you feel for her, as do I, but we don't even know for sure that she's being stalked. It could all be in her imagination. And even if she is, we've done all we can, short of moving in with her. She's taken all the precautions, so she should be safe enough, at least for now, until we know who it is."

Mallory shook her head. "I guess you're right," she said. "It's just that I... I wish... Oh, I don't know what I wish. Let's just go."

The owner of the Big Yellow Egg, Brad Lincoln, was only too pleased to show them the footage for that day and the previous evening and even made them a copy.

"She was right," Tucker said. "That's a RAV4. A late model."

They watched the footage as Jessie appeared and stood with her hands on her hips, staring at the SUV. Its windows were heavily tinted, so it was impossible to see the driver. Then, not more than a minute after Jessie had stepped outside, the SUV took off at a high rate of speed. And she'd also been right about that. It was impossible to catch a glimpse of the license plate.

"Well," Mallory said. "So much for that. What are we going to do now?"

"We're going to go back to the office, pick up the cameras, go get Annie, head to your place, and then you're going to cook us some spaghetti while I install them," he said with a big grin. "And it will, I think, be nice to have a little downtime and relax. No phones, no texts, no work. Just you, me and Annie. Sound good?"

She smiled at him and nodded. "But if she is being stalked, don't you think we should get Jessie some sort of protection, just in case?"

"We don't know for sure that she is," Tucker replied. "But I'll talk to David about it tomorrow."

She nodded dubiously, then shrugged and said, "Well… okay, I suppose."

26

WEDNESDAY, DECEMBER 11

Tucker arrived home after a pleasant evening with Mallory at just after eleven, tired but feeling better than he had in quite a while, but with a lot of questions bubbling in the back of his mind, not the least of which was his burgeoning relationship with Mallory. They hadn't spoken about it, but it had been there, hovering between them like a beautiful butterfly. When he kissed her goodnight on the porch steps, it had been just a little more than a casual peck on the lips, and he couldn't help but smile at the memory.

As usual, he woke early the following morning after a night of tossing and turning, feeling far from refreshed or revitalized and wondering what insurmountable challenges Hump Day held for them.

He lay for several moments on his back, hands behind his head, staring up at the ceiling, thinking that it was a strange situation for a private investigator to find himself in. He was potentially dealing with four police jurisdictions as well as the

FBI, and his status with all of them was unclear at best and nonexistent at worst, and it worried him; David Lewis worried him. He was smart, devious, and could be a sneaky son of a bitch whenever the mood took him. And, for once in his life, Tucker felt, professionally, out of his depth.

He sighed, rolled out of bed, went to the bathroom, turned on the shower, and slipped inside.

The hot water hammered his back like a thousand red-hot needles. He tilted his head back, closed his eyes and let the near scalding water wash over his face. For a good two minutes, he tortured himself before turning down the heat and washing his hair. Five minutes later, he stepped out of the shower, his skin still tingling, and toweled himself off.

He dressed in a pair of blue jeans and a white dress shirt, open at the neck, and then went downstairs to make coffee, only to find the jar was empty.

Damn! he thought, then sat down at the table, put his elbows on the tabletop and his hands to his temples. *That's all I need: no coffee and a headache.*

He picked up his phone and texted Mallory, *Hey you. Good morning. I hope you had a good night. Look, I'm out of coffee. Would you mind stopping by Starbucks on your way here, please?*

The reply came almost immediately. *Sure, and yes, I did have a nice night. Thank you. See you soon.*

He stared at the message for more than a minute, trying to read something into it that may or may not have been there. Finally, he set the phone down, sighed, looked at the kitchen clock, got up and went into the office and stood before the now hopelessly cluttered whiteboard, trying to make sense of it.

Mallory watched from the porch as Tucker walked to the car after kissing her goodnight. And then, with the butterflies still circling around in her stomach, she waved, turned around and walked back into the house, smiling like the cat who'd just drank a bowl full of cream. And, to say she slept well that night would have been very much the understatement.

She, too, woke early the following morning, her thoughts immediately turning to the events of the previous evening, but only for a moment.

She slipped out of bed, ran downstairs, Annie at her heels, let her out into the backyard, then made a pot of coffee and went back upstairs to shower and get dressed.

By eight, she was back downstairs. Annie had been fed, and she was ready to go to work. She decided to take Annie to work with her and was just attaching the leash when her phone beeped, indicating she had a message.

It was from Tucker. She smiled as she read it, typed a quick reply, and said, "Come on, Annie. The boss needs his morning fix."

———

Tucker stared at the images on the whiteboard, thinking there were still three Pitt Stop employees yet to be interviewed. *Or maybe only two*, he thought vaguely as he looked at the timeline. *Harrell had hernia surgery three days before Holly Wilson's murder. Could he have managed it after such a serious surgery? Huh! Maybe he could. I was thinking we could eliminate him, but maybe not; not yet, anyway. So the priority is Marks, who's off work until the weekend. And Talbot, who should be back at work today.* He stared at the photo of Holly Wilson. *There's a five-year gap between the deaths of Tiffany Delgado and Holly Wilson. Hmm, five years. What was the killer doing during those five years? Was he locked up? If he was, he isn't one of our persons of interest. Has he moved away? If so, we can again eliminate all of them. If not, what the hell was he up to? Why the break?*

His thoughts were interrupted by a knock on the door. He'd forgotten to unlock it. He opened it to find Mallory there with Annie at her heel, two Grande containers of coffee and two bags of House Blend in hand.

"Oh, thank God," he muttered, taking one of the containers from her. Then he leaned in close and kissed her gently on the lips. "Thank you. I don't think I could have lasted much longer."

"For the coffee or the kiss?" she asked as she followed him into the kitchen.

"Both," he said as he added a little milk and two packets of sweetener to the coffee. "Take a seat and let's talk."

They sat down at the table and Tucker said, "I've been thinking. Serial killers don't stop. They escalate over time. So what was our killer doing during the five years between Delgado and Wilson? Where the hell was he?"

"In prison?" she asked.

"That would be the obvious answer," Tucker replied. "And if that's it, then we've been wasting our time. It couldn't have been any of the people we've been talking to. Same goes if our killer moved out of state for five years. I think we've gotten it all wrong right from the start. What if he was still killing and we just haven't found them yet? I think we should widen our search." He sighed. "Geez, David's not going to like that."

"So what you're telling me is that none of the people we've been interviewing is the killer?"

"No, I'm not," he replied. "What I'm saying is that there's more, a lot more. How wide was your search area?"

"Southeast Tennessee and Northwest Georgia."

"Not Alabama or... Hmm. What if...? Look, we've been assuming we're looking for someone local. What if... I think we should expand the area to include Middle Tennessee, Knoxville and Northwest Alabama. What d'you think?"

"I think you're wrong," she said.

He sat back in his chair and looked at her in surprise. "You do? Why?"

"Because, if Jessie is being stalked, then it makes sense that the stalker's local."

"That doesn't make me wrong," he countered. "Our killer could be local but likes to travel. And we don't yet know for sure that Jessie's being stalked," he said, frowning.

"Well, I think she is. And I remember listening to the conversation between Holly Wilson and that Ringgold detective. She was certain she was being stalked, and she was right. And if we're not careful, Jessie is going to end up just like Holly, and I'm not going to stand by and let that happen."

Tucker stared at her, stunned. "You're serious," he said.

"Damn right I am," she replied. "We already have five victims. We have to get this guy before he kills again, and I have a deep-seated feeling that we've already talked to him, and that I'm a target. The food..." She trailed off, her eyes watering. "Tucker...?"

"Yeah, I know," he said. "I've been thinking about the food that was left on your doorstep..." He bit his top lip, wondering how he was going to handle it without upsetting her further. "And I get it, but I think maybe you're reading things..." He paused and shook his head. "Okay, look. Maybe you're right. Maybe you should stay here until we get this thing solved. I have two spare bedrooms. You can take your pick."

She shook her head. "Thank you, Tucker, but no. I have Annie, and I have my Sig, so I'll be just fine. You're right. I've been letting my imagination run away with me. People drive by and dump trash all the time."

"Not on your porch, they don't," he argued. "That was a blatant message if ever I saw one."

"Yes, well, I love my home, my fortress, and Annie and me will defend it to the death." She grinned at him, but he didn't find it funny.

"Mallory, this guy has killed five times that we know of. He's going to kill again. I don't want it to be you. Please, stay here with me where I can protect you. Just till it's over. Then you can go home."

She shook her head. "No. I'm not going to let the son of a bitch drive me out of my home. It's not going to happen. And besides, we have the cameras now."

"Whatever," he said, sounding totally frustrated. "I'm hungry. Let's go eat, then interview Larry Talbot. He should be back at work today."

"Fine," Mallory replied, "But let's go to the Big Yellow Egg. I'd like to see how Jessie's getting along, if she's even there, and I wouldn't blame her if she wasn't."

She looked at Annie, who was snoring softly in her bed.

"Annie?" The dog lifted her head and looked at her. "You be a good girl, okay?" Then to Tucker. "Maybe we should drop her off at the doggy sitter. It's not far, and I don't feel comfortable leaving her on her own."

Tucker nodded absently. Something was obviously on his mind. She grabbed the leash, hooked Annie up, and said, "Ready then?"

"What?" he asked, frowning. "Oh, yeah. Okay."

It was Jessie who served them. She seemed upbeat, but Mallory could see she wasn't doing as well as she would have them believe.

"Are you okay, Jessie?" she asked. "You're looking a little peaky."

"I'm fine," she said and was about to turn away when Mallory said, "Did you have a good night? Any… problems?"

"No. Not really," she replied. "I didn't sleep well, but I don't think I was followed. When I got home, I ran into the house and locked all the doors. I went to bed early, but…" She shook her head. "I'll go get your order."

She brought their food a few minutes later, set it down in front of them and then turned quickly away without saying a word.

"She's going to make herself sick, if she's not careful," Mallory said. "We need to catch this guy, and soon."

Tucker nodded, forked some scrambled eggs into his mouth, looked at her as he chewed, then said, "I don't know, Mallory. We have three, maybe four, persons of interest so far. And now we have victim number five, Holly Wilson. We have to rule out Raul Copper; he's in prison, which means we're left with Palmer, Watson and Gibson."

"What about Harrell, Talbot, and Marks?" she asked, consulting her notes.

"I think we can rule out Harrell for the Wilson murder. I doubt he could have killed her if he's recovering from hernia surgery, and if he didn't do that one, we can also rule him out for the other four. We still have to talk to Talbot and Marks, but I'm not liking it, Mallory. Palmer, Watson and Gibson have dodgy alibis at best. Maybe we'll have better luck with

Talbot or Marks." He heaved a sigh, shook his head and ate another bite of his eggs.

After a refill of their coffee, Tucker paid the bill, and they headed for the Pitt Stop, where they found Larry Talbot replacing a stolen catalytic convertor on a late-model Ford Explorer.

"Mr. Talbot?" Tucker said, peering under the lift.

"Yep, and you must be the two private eyes Mo told me about. What can I do for you? As if I didn't know."

"Do you have a minute?" Tucker asked.

"Sure," he said, coming out from under the lift, wiping his hands on a dirty piece of rag. "Anything for a break."

He was forty-eight, tall, slim, dark-haired, with a crooked nose and a nasty-looking scar on his chin. He was also smiling broadly.

Tucker didn't waste any time. He introduced himself and Mallory, and then said, "Would you mind telling us where you were between ten and one in the morning last Friday evening?"

"Wow," he said, frowning. "You're a bit of a hard ass, aren't you?"

Tucker didn't answer, nor did he smile. He simply stared him down.

Talbot broke eye contact, turned his head to look at Mallory, and stared at her. Then he literally looked her up and down. "I was working at home. I write romance novels." His eyes glittered, and the smile slipped a little as he continued to stare at her, then he continued, "With a little murder thrown in to make it interesting. My main character would look a lot like you, Miss Carver, if she were real."

"You were alone?" Tucker asked.

He turned again to Tucker. "I was. Sorry. See? I've been

single since early 2015. My wife divorced me. Ran off with a piece of shit from Nashville, would you believe? I'm almost always alone these days." And he turned again to look at Mallory. "How about you, Miss Carver? You dating anyone?"

"That, Mr. Talbot, is none of your business." She looked at Tucker, who took the hint.

"Two-thousand-fifteen, you say?" he said. "When?"

"April, why?"

"No reason," Tucker lied. "How did you feel about that?"

"How d'you think I felt?" He snapped. "Nineteen frickin' years we were married. Two kids. Then she starts this girl's night out crap and I find out from a buddy she's been screwin' around on me with this guy from Nashville for two years, and I didn't know a thing about it. How the hell would you feel?"

Tucker stared at him for a moment, then said, "I'd feel pretty pissed off, and I'd want to get back at her. Is that how you felt, Mr. Talbot?"

"Yes... I... did, but as soon as I found out about it, she hightailed it to him in Nashville. Took the kids with her. They've been together ever since. I ain't seen my kids in more'n two years."

"So you were pretty angry then?"

"Yeah, I was angry. I'm still frickin' angry. Wouldn't you be?"

Tucker ignored the question and said, "Angry enough to kill?"

"Are you frickin' kidding me?" he asked, seemingly outraged by the question.

Tucker shook his head. "No, Mr. Talbot. I'm not kidding. Did you by any chance know a Miss Elaine May? She was a prostitute. She lived in Cleveland in 2015."

He frowned, looked away, and shook his head. "You don't

have to shade it, Mr. Randall. I know who she was. She was Mo's girlfriend. He told me all about her and what happened to her. I met her a couple of times. She was murdered. But I never had anything to do with her, if you get my meanin'. See, I don't pay for it. I don't have to. I have friends, lady friends." He turned his head to look at Mallory and… it was more a sneer than a smile and inwardly Mallory shuddered.

"Hey," Tucker said, noticing the look he was giving her. "How about Bernice Carr?"

He turned again to Tucker and said, "Yeah, Mo told me about her, too, but I never met her. Look, I know you've been poking around here talking to all the other employees. I didn't kill nobody. I just work here every day, and I've never been in no trouble, not for nothin'… Ever!"

How about Franny McNeer from Polk County?" Tucker persisted, watching him closely. "Did you know her?"

He made a face and shook his head.

"Tiffany Delgado, Ringgold?"

Again, he shook his head.

"All right, Mr. Talbot," he said. "I think we're done here. We'll be in touch." He looked at Mallory and said, "Let's go."

And they did. They went into the convenience store where the guy Pete was behind the counter doing something on his phone.

"Oh, hey. Hi," he said after looking up at them. He straightened up. "What can I do for you today? More questions?"

"No," Tucker replied. "We were just wondering if you know where we can find Jarred Marks. I know he's off until the weekend, but…?" He left the question open.

"He's gone fishing. Lake Eufaula, Alabama, I think. He should be back on Friday, late. I shouldn't wonder."

"Good to know. Thanks," Tucker said and turned to go.

"Have a nice day."

Tucker turned, but Pete was already hunched over his phone again. Tucker shook his head and smiled, and together they walked back to the car.

"I did not like that guy Talbot," Mallory said as she opened the car door. "I think he's a real possibility." She slid into the passenger seat and pulled the door closed. "He obviously hates women."

Any other time, Tucker would have played devil's advocate, but this time he had little to say other than to agree. "You could be right," he replied, "but that doesn't make him a killer."

"He's the most likely prospect we've talked to yet," she persisted.

"I think we need to know more about him," he replied.

"But he knew Elaine and Bernice, and his wife left him in April, and Elaine was murdered in July, just three months later. Is that a coincidence? I don't think so."

"You really don't like him, do you?" Tucker asked, glancing sideways at her.

"No, I don't. And did you see the way he was looking at me? It made my skin crawl... What are you going to tell David?"

"Nothing yet. In fact, I wish to hell he'd gather his crap and go on back to where he came from."

"Oh, come on, Tucker. Get over it. I think he's nice."

"Not too nice, I hope. What have you got planned for tonight? I was thinking Mexican."

She blew out through her lips, thought about it for a moment, and then said, "Not tonight, if you don't mind. I was thinking maybe I should have an early night. You could probably use one, too. Or... Maybe... you... could... come over," she finished shyly.

He thought for a moment, then said, "You know, I'd love to. I really would, but you're right; we both need an early night. How about if I come over tomorrow night instead?"

"That sounds lovely," she said. "Thank you, Tucker."

As it turned out, though, at a little after five-thirty that afternoon, David Lewis called Tucker and invited himself over for a beer and a chat—just a chat. Not to talk about the case.

Tucker reluctantly agreed, and David arrived an hour later with a twelve-pack of Modello.

27

It was a little after six-thirty when Mallory arrived home with Annie that Wednesday evening, and it was almost totally dark. After she unlocked the front door, they stepped inside, and Mallory turned and set both the lock and the deadbolt Tucker had installed. That done, she followed Annie to the back door, unlocked it, opened it and let Annie out. She was about to close the door and let Annie do her thing when she saw the dog running back and forth on the deck, her nose to the boards; then she went to the steps, went into a low crouch and began to growl.

Mallory, who'd already been thinking about the sack of food someone had left on the front porch, froze, the hair on the back of her neck prickling.

"Stay, Annie," she whispered, backing into the house.

She grabbed her purse from the kitchen table, opened it and took out the compact nine-millimeter pistol, checked the safety and the load, grabbed a flashlight from the kitchen counter, and then stepped cautiously out onto the back deck.

If it's him and he's still out there, I'll get him, she thought. *He's into knives, not guns.*

"Annie, go seek," she whispered, and the dog took off down the steps into the backyard, heading toward the trees that bounded her property.

Mallory took a deep breath, bit her bottom lip, and then followed Annie into the darkness, waving the flashlight back and forth as she went. It wasn't until she'd almost reached the boundary that she spotted Annie almost hidden by the long grass, sniffing and pawing at something on the ground.

"Annie, bring it to me!" she shouted. It was a command with which Annie was entirely familiar, having learned it as a puppy playing with her toys.

She pawed whatever it was some more, grabbed it between her jaws, then turned and trotted back to Mallory.

Mallory frowned when she saw what it was. "Bring it to me, Annie," she repeated, holding out her hand.

The dog obediently placed it gently in her hand.

"Good girl," she said as she shone the flashlight onto what appeared to be a pocket-size notebook. She turned it over and looked at the back, thinking it couldn't have been there long. The air was damp from the low-lying mist over the fields beyond her property, but the notebook was perfectly dry.

"Come on, Annie," she said, looking around, playing the beam of the flashlight back and forth over the trees and the fields but seeing nothing out of the ordinary. Together, they walked the path back to the house, mounted the three steps up onto the deck and there she stopped, staring at the partially open door, unable to remember if she'd closed it or not.

After a moment's thought, she decided she'd left it open.

She looked down at Annie. She seemed perfectly at ease now, looking up at her, panting gently.

She went back inside, locked the door, absentmindedly staring at one of the pages in the notebook as she filled Annie's bowl with food, and then sat down at the kitchen table and began to flip through the pages. It was small but thick, measuring roughly four-by-six-by-one, with perhaps a hundred pages, and all but a dozen of them filled with small, but neat, cursive handwriting, and she was stunned by what she read. Page after page was filled with the private information of dozens of women, including age, description, address, phone number, social security number, even credit card numbers complete with the three-digit security codes. Each entry was dated, going back to January 2019. One by one, she flipped through the pages until she came to the one headed Tiffany Delgado, which she read in detail. What horrified her most was that Tiffany's name had been crossed out in red and the date, August 9, 2019, written in the margin.

Mallory bit her bottom lip, knowing exactly what that meant and what she was looking at. She flipped through the rest of the pages, almost to the end, until she read Holly Wilson. It, too, was crossed out in red ink and the date December 6, 2024, written in the margin. But it was when she turned to the final few pages that her blood turned to ice water. The penultimate entry was for Jessie Mills. It hadn't been crossed out, but the date December 11, 2024, had been written in the margin. *Oh, my God.* She thought. *That's today.* She was about to jump to her feet when she realized there was one more entry. She turned the page and, sure enough, there it was, Mallory Carver.

There was no date in the margin, but the information was

all there, all but her credit card information, and she wondered why it wasn't.

She sat for a moment, staring at her name. Then she looked up at the clock. It was a little after seven-thirty. *Oh geez! What was I thinking?* She jumped up from the table, grabbed her keys, phone and gun, told Annie to stay and be a good girl, then ran to the door, opened it, set the lock and flung it closed behind her. She ran down the porch steps to her car, started the engine, backed out onto the street, and peeled away, heading for Jessie Mills' home.

And then she called Tucker. It was seven-forty-five.

28

It was almost seven o'clock when David arrived at Tucker's door with a twelve-pack of Modello and a paper sack containing two Subway sandwiches.

"I thought you might like something to eat," he said as he set both down on the kitchen table. "How was your day?"

"So-so," Tucker replied. "How was yours?"

"Unproductive," he replied as they sat down at the table and began to unwrap the sandwiches. "I thought you might like turkey and Swiss on rye. And Modello is always a good choice, right?"

"What d'you want, David?" Tucker said dryly. "I know you well enough to know you never do anything without a motive."

"That's the Tucker I remember. Ever the optimist," he replied sarcastically. "I don't want anything other than a quiet, catch-up evening with my old friend and partner. No talk about the case. Just a chat and a pleasant evening."

Tucker shook his head, opened two bottles of beer, pushed one across the table to the FBI agent, stared at him for a moment, then said, "Let's get things straight, David. You were never my friend, and I was never your partner. I was your go-to when you needed dirty work done. So cut the crap and tell me why you're really here."

"Now that's just not true," David said before taking a sip of beer. "I always thought of our relationship as mentor and mentee." He shrugged. "And, by the look of things, I did a pretty good job…" he said, looking around. "And, talking about pretty, where's that lovely partner of yours? I was hoping she'd be here, too. Lovely girl, that. Where d'you find her? Or did she find you?"

"She's at home. Where d'you think she'd be?" Tucker asked, his hackles raising. "And how I found her, as you put it, is no damn business of yours."

"Calm down, Tucker. I meant no harm, but having seen how you two respond to each other, I would have thought you'd have moved her in with you." He grinned at him.

"As usual, you've gotten it all wrong, David," Tucker snapped. "Mallory and I are business partners. No more than that."

"Bullshit," David said, leaning back in his chair. "The woman's in love with you. Anyone can see that by the way she looks at you, and you at her, for that matter."

Tucker was stunned. *Geez, is it that obvious?*

Obviously, it was, but he denied it again, anyway. "As I said, you've gotten it all wrong, just as you always do, just as you did with Marsha Cline," he said, deftly changing the subject.

"Marsha Cline!" David said. "There you go again, Tucker. For God's sake, please get over it…" He stared at him, bottle in hand, and then continued, "And that's why you decided to quit, isn't it? You know, that's one thing I would never have believed of you, Tucker, that you're a quitter."

"Why don't you just take your—"

But it was at that moment that Tucker was cut off before he could finish the sentence when his phone rang. He glanced at the screen. *Mallory? What the...*

He picked up the phone. "Mallory—?"

"Tucker, you've got to come. I found a notebook in the backyard—well Annie found it—but it's full of stuff about the victims. It must belong to the killer. He must have dropped it. He's stalking me, too—"

"Slow down, Mallory," Tucker said. "I can't understand a word you're saying."

"I'm saying you need to meet me at Jessie's house," she yelled. "He's going to kill her. Tonight. Then he's going to kill me. It's all in the notebook. The victims, the dates, everything."

"Not if I have anything to say about it," Tucker growled. "Where the hell are you, Mallory?"

"I'm in the damn car," she yelled. "Where d'you think I am? I'm on my way to Jessie's house. You've got to come. He's going to kill her, Tucker. Tonight. He might already be there."

"Mallory. Stop. I'm at least thirty minutes away from Jessie's home. You've got to wait for me. Do not go to that house by yourself. Do you understand?"

"Yes, but—"

"Stop it, Mallory. Who is it? Who are we dealing with?"

"I don't know who it is. Tucker, the notebook is full of information about the victims, everything. Tiffany, Holly, Jessie, me. But there's nothing in it about the killer. Are you coming?"

"Yes, I'm on my way," he replied as he jumped to his feet. "Mallory, do not go without me. Do you hear me?"

Mallory babbled something he couldn't understand and then the phone went dead.

Damn it, he thought savagely. She hung up. She's doing it. She's going there alone. She doesn't know what the hell she's doing or what she's getting herself into.

By then he was on his feet. "Come on, David. You're coming with me." He grabbed his jacket and his gun and turned to David, who was also on his feet.

"What's going on, Tucker?" he asked. "I heard some of that, but what I'm getting is that Mallory knows who the killer is and is on her way to Jessie Mill's home. Yes?"

"Yeah," Tucker replied. "Come on. We need to hurry and get there before she gets herself into more trouble than she can handle. We'll talk in the car."

They'd been in the car for five minutes with Tucker driving like he was insane and not saying a word before David finally shouted, "Are you going to tell me what the hell's going on?"

"I'm not entirely sure," Tucker answered, his knuckles white on the wheel. "It seems Mallory's dog found a notebook with a lot of names and information in it, including some of the victims, including hers and Jessie Mills. She thinks she's being stalked and that whoever it is the notebook belongs to is going to kill Mills tonight, and she's on her way to stop him. She's going to get herself killed if we don't get there fast."

"Holy shit!" David whispered. "That changes everything. D'you think it's legit?"

"If she said she found it, she found it," Tucker replied as the speedometer crept past seventy. "As to the information... who the hell knows? But I think we're about to find out. Oh, shit!" he growled, looking up at the rearview mirror.

"What? What's wrong?"

"We've got ourselves a tail, a cop."

As he said it, the red and blue lights on the car behind began to flash and the siren wail.

Tucker pulled over, put the car in park, rolled down the window, put both hands on the wheel and waited, tapping the wheel with his fingers in frustration.

"In a bit of a hurry, weren't we, sir?" the cop said, leaning forward, his right hand on the butt of his gun.

Tucker was about to answer, but David beat him to it, leaning across the console, offering his creds to the officer.

"Special Agent David Lewis," he barked at the officer. "We have an emergency. There's possibly a crime in progress. We need backup. Call it in, please. The address is…" He looked at Tucker.

Tucker nodded and gave the officer Jessie's address.

The officer handed David's creds back, nodded, and ran back to his car while Tucker put the car in drive and pulled out onto the street.

"Thanks, David," he muttered. "I wouldn't have gotten away with that."

"You're welcome, Tucker. Now let's do this, yeah?"

Tucker nodded grimly and said, "Yeah!"

29

It was a little after eight when Mallory arrived outside Jessie Mills' house. There was no garage, so she assumed the older model Honda Accord parked in the driveway must belong to Jessie, which was a good sign.

She looked up at the rearview mirror and saw the street behind her was empty, then she looked ahead through the windshield. A dark-colored SUV was parked about half a block away on the same side of the road, and other driveways had cars in them, but that was all. Nobody was creeping around, no cars were moving, and she didn't see any headlights approaching. The area looked safe, so she heaved a sigh of relief, turned off the engine, stepped out of the car and stood for a moment, listening. All was quiet. The air still. Mallory hesitated, wondering what to do, looking back and forth, up and down the street. *Tucker said to wait,* she thought. *But what if...*

She looked up at Jessie's bedroom window. The lights were on, and the drapes were closed, but she could see shadows moving inside, then... She furrowed her brow, listening. *She's not on her own... Ooh, what was that?* she thought. *It sounded like a scream. Oh, my God. He's already here.*

She fumbled for her phone. Dropped it. Picked it up and hit the speed dial for Tucker.

"Where are you?" she screamed. "He's here. He's already inside. He's killing her."

"We're about ten minutes out," Tucker shouted. "The police are on their way. Stay where you are. Do not attempt to go inside."

"But he's killing her, Tucker. I can't just stand here and do nothing."

"You'll do exactly what—" but she'd already hung up.

Mallory ran to the front door, her P938 in her hand. She tried the doorknob. The door was locked. She heard another scream. She backed away from the door, looked up. The bedroom lights were still on, but as far as she could see, nothing was moving. She ran around to the back of the house. A window was ajar. She hesitated only for a second, then crawled into the house. She could hear screaming upstairs.

"Jessie, Jessie, Jessie," she yelled at the top of her voice as she ran to the stairs and then up, taking them two at a time. The bedroom door was busted wide open, and she could hear sounds of a struggle and someone whimpering.

"Jessie," she shouted again as she ran to the bedroom door. Jessie was on the floor, on one elbow between the bed and the window, a figure dressed in black on top of her, their arm raised, knife in hand, about to stab her. Her right arm was raised, her forearm in front of her face as if to ward off the blow.

"Back off, you son of a bitch," Mallory yelled and fired a shot that hit the wall just above the figure's head.

The figure reared up, turned, stared at her, then threw

the knife at Mallory. She ducked. It bounced off the wall beside the door and fell to the floor. She froze as the figure hurled itself over the bed, grabbed her arm, and slammed it against the edge of the open door. The gun flew out of her fingers, skittered across the hardwood floor and slid under the bed.

"You frickin' bitch," a male voice screamed in her ear. "I almost had her. Why d'you have to stick your stupid nose in where it don't belong?"

He threw her to the ground, jumped on top of her, and reached across her for the knife. She slammed her fist into the side of his face as hard as she could. He grunted and hammered his fist into her jaw. Pain seared through her head. She almost blacked out. She went for his eyes with both hands and managed to press her right thumb to his left eye. He screeched, twisted his head away, grabbed her hand and wrenched it away from his eye, then hit her again in the face. She rolled sideways. He was in mid-swing at her and lost his balance. She clawed at his face and only managed to grab the balaclava, but she ripped it from his head and found herself staring at a familiar face.

"You frickin' bitch," he yelled. "I'm going to frickin' kill you now. I was going to anyway, but you couldn't wait, could you, you stupid bitch? You just couldn't wait."

"You!" she yelped. "It's you!"

"Of course it's me, you frickin stupid…" He trailed off and punched her in the face again, and then again, and then again, all the while looking wildly around, searching for the knife. He spotted it, reached for it, but before he could grab it, she grabbed him between his legs and squeezed as hard as she could.

He squealed and backhanded her with all his might. Her

head snapped back, connected hard with the edge of the door, and everything went black.

He sat back on his heels, rocking back and forth, breathing hard, his left eye closed, his right eye watering, nursing his genitals, staring at her. "Frickin' bitch," he muttered. Then he lost it and screamed, "Bitch, bitch, bitch." He slapped her face as hard as he could. "Bitch!" And he slapped her again. "You hear me, bitch?" he yelled.

She heard nothing, and she felt nothing. She was unconscious. A deep wound to the back of her head.

He slapped her again. Her head rolled from one side to the other. He reached over, almost fell off her, grabbed the knife, turned again to the still unconscious Mallory, raised it over his head with both hands, paused for a second and snarled, "Your turn now, bitch!"

BAM! And before he could blink, something slammed into his left shoulder. He tipped over backward, the knife flying from his fingers. His head slammed into the footboard of the bed and, for several seconds, he seemed to lose consciousness. He blinked several times with his good eye, coughed, rolled over onto his stomach, then tried to sit up.

"You," he said, staring at Tucker who was down on one knee beside Mallory, gun in hand, pointing at him, two fingers of his left hand at her throat, feeling for a pulse.

"You!" Tucker snarled. "If you've—"

"Yeah, fooled y'all, didn't I?" He grinned at Tucker through gritted teeth, his hand on his wounded shoulder. "I wondered when you'd catch on, but you didn't, did you? You never would have. I had y'all fooled. Even that silly bitch didn't know until she pulled my frickin' hood off. Dumbasses, all of you. Geez, it frickin' hurts. I ain't never been shot before. Why didn't you kill me, Randall? You couldn't have missed, close as you were. Is she dead?"

Tucker shook his head. "I didn't kill you because I wanted to make sure you suffer for what you've done. And no, she isn't dead, and you'd better pray she doesn't die, because if she does—"

"You'll do what?" he asked, cutting him off and grinning at him. "You can't do a damn thing, Randall. I'm in the system now, and it will protect me." He paused for a second, looking at Mallory, then continued, "A few seconds more and I would've had her. I hate people like her. Arrogant, stupid bitches, all of 'em." He looked up at David, who was standing in the doorway. "Who's your friend?"

"Your worst nightmare," Tucker snarled.

"Who is he?" David asked, standing in the doorway, also with a gun in his hand.

"Pete Abbott, from the Pitt Stop. Boy, did I ever get that one wrong? Did you call an ambulance?"

"Yeah, they're on their way," he replied. "Where's Jessie Mills?" He was looking at Abbott.

"Over there," Abbott said. "Other side of the bed."

"She dead?"

Abbott shrugged, winced, closed his good eye, then opened it and said, "I sure as hell hope so… Frickin' hell, I think that frickin' bitch has put my eye out."

But Jessie wasn't dead. She was lying on her side with her hands covering her ears. Her face was covered in blood, and she was crying.

"Jessie," David said gently, holding out a hand.

She opened her eyes and looked up at him, blood streaming from a deep knife wound to the left side of her head where Abbott's knife had slid by as she'd jerked her head away.

She didn't answer. Instead, she reached out, took his hand, and he helped her to her knees. Then he put his arm around her and helped her to her feet. Jessie staggered painfully to the door, where she stopped and looked down at Mallory.

"She saved my life," she whispered. "Is she going to be all right?"

Tucker looked up at her, closed his eyes, opened them again, and nodded. "I hope so. I sure as hell hope so."

30

THURSDAY, DECEMBER 12

It was almost nine the following morning when Mallory woke up. She opened her eyes and stared up at the brightly lit white ceiling. And she knew almost immediately that she was in the hospital. She lay there for a moment with her eyes closed, feeling comfortable and a little euphoric, wondering what had happened to her.

She opened her eyes again, turned her head a little to the right, closed them again and winced as pain speared through her head. She waited until it dissipated, then opened her eyes again and smiled. Tucker was asleep at her bedside, and he was holding her hand.

She closed her eyes again, still smiling, and was almost asleep when she heard a voice that said, "Tucker?"

She opened her eyes and saw David Lewis standing at the foot of the bed.

"Hey, Mallory," he said. "You're awake—"

"What?" Tucker, suddenly awake, sat up and let go of Mallory's hand, his face flushing.

Mallory scoffed, reached out, and took his hand again.

Tucker looked at her, then at David.

"I guess I dozed off," Tucker said.

"Could I have some water?" Mallory asked, her voice cracked and dry.

"Yes, of course." Tucker rose quickly and rounded the bed and David to get it for her.

"Can you sit me up a bit, please?"

"Yeah… Yes," he said, searching for the control unit.

He raised the head of the bed and handed her a cup with a lid and a straw.

She sipped some ice water, closed her eyes and sipped again, then she looked up at him, smiled and handed him the cup.

Tucker rounded the bed again and sat down.

"What happened?" she asked. "Did you get him? Is Jessie all right? And, Tucker, just so you know, I recorded the whole thing."

"You got yourself into one hell of a scrap," he replied. "Abbott beat you pretty badly. You have a concussion, but the doc says it will pass over the next couple of days. But yes, we got him. And Jessie's all right, too. She's in a room just down the hall."

He looked at David. "What's the word on Abbott?"

"He's here. The wound was through and through. What ammo were you using?"

"FMJ," Tucker replied ruefully. "Full metal jacket."

"A bit chancy, that, don't you think?" David asked.

"An oversight," Tucker replied. "Range rounds. My bad."

David nodded. "You look like hell, Tucker," he said. "You've been here all night?"

Tucker merely nodded.

Mallory turned her head to look at him and said, "Thank you, Tucker. You should go home now. I'll be fine."

Tucker wrinkled his brow, looked at David and said, "So, what about Abbott? Have you interviewed him yet?"

"No. I was waiting to see if he'd be fit enough. The surgeon says the wound is clean, no internal damage, so they patched him up and will turn him loose this afternoon. He's officially in my custody, but he'll be released to the Chattanooga PD. I've arranged to interview him there. I'd like you to attend. You up for it?" David asked.

Tucker looked at Mallory. She smiled at him and nodded.

"Oh, yeah," he said. "You bet."

"Good," David said. "I'll leave you two alone, then." He looked at Tucker and said, "Two o'clock. Amnicola Highway."

"I know where it is, David... Thanks."

David nodded and turned and left the room.

"How are you feeling?" Tucker asked as the door closed behind him.

"Not so hot," she replied. "I must look a mess."

"Eh, not so bad for someone with a bandage around her head, a split lip, two broken ribs and multiple bruises. Why did you do it, Mallory? I told you to wait for me."

"Yes, I know you did, and I was going to, but I could hear Jessie screaming and a window was open and... Tucker, he was just about to stab her when I got there. I had to do something, so I shot at him and missed. I was nervous, I guess. Did you find my Sig? He knocked it out of my hand. It went under the bed and—" She burst into tears.

"Hey, come on," Tucker said. "You did great." He wanted to put his arm around her, but with the IV and the monitor cables he couldn't, so he took her hand in both of his and kissed it.

"No, I didn't," she blubbered. "I almost got myself killed. If you hadn't arrived when you did…"

"Stop it, Mallory," he said, then rose to his feet, leaned over the bed and kissed her.

The door opened. "Ah, feeling better, are we?"

Tucker sat down again. "Doctor," he said.

"So, how are you feeling?" she said to Mallory.

"I'm good," she replied. "When can I go home… Oh, geez, Tucker. Annie!"

"She's fine," he replied. "I called your sister. She went by this morning and let her out and fed her. She'd peed on the kitchen floor, I'm afraid. But Jen cleaned it up. I'll go by when I leave here. So stop worrying. Oh, and by the way…" He looked at his watch. "She'll be here in about ten minutes." He looked at the doctor.

"Hmm," she said, looking at her iPad. You have a mild concussion, two cracked ribs and quite a bit of bruising. Other than that… D'you have anyone at home?"

"She does," Tucker said, jumping in before Mallory could answer. "Me."

Mallory almost choked, trying to suppress her surprise.

The doctor looked at him over her glasses, frowning, then looked at Mallory, who was blushing. The frown deepened. "Well, I suppose… We'll see how the rest of the day goes. If all goes well, she can go home this evening." With that, she nodded, turned on her heel, and left the room.

She hadn't been gone more than two minutes when Jen burst into the room. She took one look at her sister, then said,

"Oh, my God, Mallory. What the hell happened? What were you thinking?"

"You've been talking to Tucker," Mallory accused her.

"Damn right, I have. Have you gone mad, taking that monster on by yourself? What were you thinking?" she repeated.

Mallory shrugged, winced, and wished she hadn't. "I couldn't let him kill her, now could I?" she replied.

Jen looked at Tucker. "And you can wipe that silly grin off your face. Mallory, I just spoke with your doctor and you're coming home with me this evening."

"Er… no!" Mallory replied. "Thank you, Jen, but I want to go home."

"But—"

"I said I want to go home," Mallory said gently.

Jen looked at Tucker. "Is this your doing?"

Tucker just shrugged.

"The doctor said she has to have someone… with… her… Oh, I see. That's how it is, is it?"

At that, Tucker stood and said, "I have to go. You two decide who does what and let me know."

He bent over the bed and kissed Mallory, who put her hand to his neck. "Call me later," he whispered. Then he turned to Jen, winked at her and walked quickly out of the room.

Jen stared after him, then at her sister. "Seriously?" she asked. "When did that happen?"

Mallory shrugged again and winced.

"Is it serious?" Jen asked.

"I don't know," Mallory replied. "We haven't really talked about it yet."

"Have you…"

Mallory frowned at her. "*No*. Of course not."

"Just asking," Jen said and sat down in the chair Tucker had just vacated. "So, tell me all about it."

31

David met Tucker in the front parking lot of the Chattanooga Police Service Center on Amnicola Highway and escorted him inside.

"How's Mallory?" he asked as he followed Tucker through the glass doors.

"Last time I spoke to her, she was eager to come home."

"What's your relationship with her?" he asked after he'd signed Tucker in.

"That's none of your business, David."

"I was just asking, is all," the FBI agent said.

"Why? What's it to you?"

"Well, I was hoping I could talk you into coming back to us."

"Not a chance, David," he replied. "I have a good life now, and besides, I hate the damn bureaucracy. I have no one to answer to. I make my own decisions, take only the cases that interest me. As I said, it's a good life."

"Will you think about it?" David asked. "You can pick up where you left off."

Tucker stopped walking. "Are you serious?"

David had taken another couple of steps before stopping and turning to look at him. "Of course," he replied, not catching the tenor of Tucker's question. "Same deal, same pay grade. It will be as if you never left."

Tucker shook his head in amazement. "I can't believe you'd say that. Not after what happened. You may have gotten over Marsha, but I haven't. No, I will *not* think about it. Now let it go and let's do what we're here for."

"Okay," David said. "Your loss, my friend."

Tucker was about to respond to that, but he gritted his teeth and together they walked to the interrogation room, where Peter Abbott was already waiting for them with his attorney.

Abbott was dressed in an orange jumpsuit and wearing a full set of chains, including leg cuffs. His right hand was hand-cuffed to the table with his attorney, a blonde woman Tucker knew slightly named Helena Charles, at his side.

How ironic, Tucker thought. *The woman could have been one of his victims.*

"Here they are," Abbott, his arm in a sling, said brightly, looking up at them. "No energy drink today, Mr. Randall?"

Tucker looked at him and shook his head in disbelief. He and David took their seats on the opposite side of the table to Abbott and his attorney.

Abbott clamped his lips together in a tight smile, looked from one to the other and then said, "So?"

David began the interview by announcing the date, time, and those present. "Interview of Peter Abbott, December 12, 2024, at two-seventeen p.m. Present are Mr. Abbott, his attorney Ms. Helena Charles, FBI Special Agent in Charge

David Lewis and Detective Tucker Randall. Also present is corrections officer Michael Grady."

He paused, staring at Abbott. Abbott, his head tilted to one side, stared back at him, the same tight smile on his lips.

What the hell is he thinking? Tucker wondered.

"Peter Abbott," David began, "I'm charging you with the attempted murders of Jessie Ann Mills and Mallory Carver. You have the right to remain silent. Anything you say can and will be used against you in a court of law. You have the right to talk to a lawyer for advice before we ask you any questions. You have the right to have a lawyer with you during questioning. If you cannot afford a lawyer, one will be appointed for you before any questioning if you wish. If you decide to answer questions now without a lawyer present, you have the right to stop answering at any time. Do you understand these rights?"

Still smiling, Abbott looked at Charles. She nodded, and he replied, "Yes, but I wasn't trying to kill her."

"Seriously—" Tucker began, leaning forward, but David put a hand on his arm and cut him off.

"Would you like to explain that statement, Mr. Abbott?" David asked.

"I wasn't trying to kill her," he repeated. "It was the other way round. She was trying to kill me. See, I met her at the store a couple of weeks ago. She came beboppin' in all uppity, like, and we kinda hit it off, you know? I just went to her house to see if I could ask her out. She invited me in and, well, I must have said something to set her off because she just went nuts, grabbed a knife from the drawer and went for me."

Tucker looked at him, not believing what he was hearing.

David merely nodded and said, "So, you were in the kitchen when this happened?"

Abbott thought for a minute, then grinned and said, "No, the bedroom."

"So, Jessie Mills, a woman you barely knew, invited you into the house, then up to the bedroom, where she took a kitchen knife from one of her drawers and attempted to stab you?"

"That's about the size of it," he said.

David nodded and said, "Please continue, Mr. Abbott."

"Well, I had to defend myself, didn't I? We fought, and I was able to get the knife away from her and—"

"Bullshit," Tucker snapped. "I'll tell *you* what happened. You saw her in the store as you said, just as you did all the other women you killed, and you stalked her. You broke into her house through a window. She was in the bedroom where you attacked her. But, unlike the other women, she fought you, didn't she, Pete? Would you like to know how I know all that?" He didn't wait for an answer. He slammed the notebook, sealed in a plastic evidence bag, down on the table. "Recognize it?" he asked. "You should. It has your fingerprints all over it."

Abbott stared at it. Tucker watched as his face paled.

"Where d'you get that?" he whispered.

Charles put a hand on his arm and shook her head. He shrugged her hand away.

"You dropped it in Mallory Carver's backyard. It was you who put the paper sack of fast food on her doorstep, too, wasn't it?"

He hesitated for a second, then said, "I've never seen that before."

"Really?" Tucker said, taking a pair of latex gloves from his pocket. "Let's see, shall we?"

He snapped on the gloves, broke the seal on the envelope,

took out the notebook, opened it and rifled through the pages. "Ah, here we are. Jessie Mills, December 11, and here are all her private and personal details. Why December 11, Pete?"

"That was..." He realized his mistake, closed his mouth and folded his arms.

"You were going to say that was the date you met her, weren't you? But you just said you met her a couple of weeks ago, during which time you were able to gather all this information, so why December 11?" Abbott didn't answer. He just stared stoically at Tucker. "But there's more, isn't there, Pete? Let's try this one. Holly Wilson? Remember her?"

Abbott stirred uncomfortably in his chair but said nothing.

Tucker nodded and pressed on, "Now that one is a little different. It's dated December 6, the day she was murdered, and look at this." He showed the entry to Abbott, Charles, and then David. "Her name has been crossed out in red. What does that mean, Pete? You entered the date you intended to kill her, didn't you? Then, when you had, you crossed out her name."

"Let's take a look at another one." He flipped through the pages, then looked up at him and said, "Tiffany Delgado, August 9, 2016. Same thing. The name's crossed out in red. And how about this one, Mallory Carver? No date yet, but the intention is clear, isn't it, Pete? And not only are your fingerprints all over it, but a handwriting expert will testify you wrote it all—"

"Okay, okay, okay," Abbott shouted. "That's enough. I did it. I killed—"

"Stop!" his lawyer shouted, grabbing his arm.

"Get off," he shouted, snatching his arm away from her. "I killed 'em, and I would have killed the Mills woman, too, if that silly bitch hadn't charged in when she did. So what? They deserved it. All of them stupid blonde bitches. I frickin' hate women. They're sneaky, conniving, sly, shitty bitches, especially the blonde ones. They're the worst. Just like my mother was, frickin' bitch. And where the hell did they dig you up from?" He turned to his attorney and continued his rant. "You're just like the rest of them. Lousy, lying bitches. Do your frickin' worst. I don't give a shit."

It was at that moment Officer Grady stepped forward to restrain him, but David held up a hand.

"So," he said, after Abbott had seen Grady, a huge man, step forward and he'd calmed down, "you admit to the attempted murders of Jessie Mills and Mallory Carver?"

He nodded.

"Say it, please, Mr. Abbott, for the recording."

"Yes, damn you. Yes!" he snarled.

"And you admit to the murders of Tiffany Delgado and Holly Jennifer Wilson?"

Again, he nodded, then, almost as an afterthought. "Yup!" And then he reverted to the tight smile and folded his arms across his chest and leaned back in his chair, staring at them, waiting.

"How about Elaine May?"

"Ah, pretty little Elaine, Mo's lover," he said, staring at the far wall. "She was the first. She was always in and out of the store. Beboppin' around in those tiny little skirts and halter tops. She'd screw anything with a pulse if they had enough money, women included. She was a hooker, you know?"

"You stabbed her thirty-seven times," David said. "Why so brutal? One or two would have done the job."

"Thirty-seven, was it? I didn't count. I guess I must have gotten lost in the moment." He grinned at Tucker. "That *associate* of yours," he said with a sneer, "the Carver woman; you screwin' her, Detective?"

Tucker jumped to his feet, but David grabbed his arm, restraining him. "Easy does it," he said, and Tucker slowly sat down again.

"How did you gain entry to May's home?" Tucker asked.

"Easy enough," he replied. "Old house, old windows. I went in through one at the rear. I just had to slip a Slim-Jim between the two sashes and push the catch to the side. She was asleep on the couch." He smiled at the memory. "You should have seen her face when I woke her. I'll remember that look for the rest of my days."

The two detectives were silent for a moment, then David said, "And Bernice Carr?"

Again, Abbott made with the tight smile and nodded, then said, "Bernie, Mo's cousin. Yep, her too. She was always in and around the store. What more can I say?"

"How about Frances McNeer, Franny? Did you kill her, too?"

At that, he burst out laughing. "Now that one was a trip—"

"A trip?" Tucker asked, horrified. "You stabbed that poor woman forty-seven times, you frickin' monster."

"Forty-seven, was it? I guess I must have been in a bad mood that day. Hmm, I remember the day she came into the store... she only came in once. There was... something about her... I dunno. I never did figure it out. She... just... Eh," he frowned. "I don't know. As I said, there was just something about her that didn't sit well with me."

"So you decided to kill her," Tucker pressed him.

"Yeah, I suppose I did, but here's the kicker. Here's why I said it was a trip. They convicted her dumbass husband for it and sent him away for life. Can you believe that? That was a turn-on, believe me."

"So something about Franny McNeer didn't sit well with you, so you killed her?" Tucker pressed, trying to make sure he got a viable confession from him.

"I know what you're doing, Detective, so let me help you out here." He uncrossed his arms and leaned forward. "Yes, I killed, murdered, Frances McNeer. There. Feel better now?"

Tucker took a deep breath and leaned back in his chair. He had what he wanted. And, internally, he was elated. Luthor McNeer would go free.

David glanced at Tucker, then looked at Abbott and said, "How many more, Pete?"

"Ah-hah," Abbott replied. "Now there's the question. What makes you think there are more?"

"You say Elaine May was first, then you waited almost a year before you killed Bernice Carr and then Franny McNeer three months later, but there was no one between May and Bernice."

"There wasn't?" Abbott asked. "What makes you say that?"

"So there was?" David asked.

"Was there?" Abbott replied, grinning.

"Okay, we'll come back to that later," David said. He sounded frustrated. "There was a three-year gap between the murder of Franny McNeer and Tiffany Delgado. There were none during that time either," he said.

"Weren't there?" Abbott asked, beaming at him. "Okay, so here's the thing—"

At that point, Helena Charles again put her hand on his arm and tried to stop him from talking, but he was having none of it. He shrugged her hand away and said, "Stop it, you silly bitch. Can't you see it's over? Just sit there quietly and listen or piss off. Now, where was I? Oh yes. So, here's the thing. I'm not stupid, Agent Lewis. I know interstate murder is a federal capital offense, and I could be sentenced to death. So I want a deal. You promise to take the death sentence off the table—and I want it in writing—and I'll tell you about the rest. Who they are and where they are. Deal?" He looked at Helena. She nodded and looked at David, her eyebrows raised in question.

David nodded and said, "I can't promise—"

"Then you don't get the others," Abbott said, cutting him off.

"How many?" David asked.

Abbott leaned forward, his eyes narrowed to mere slits, and said, "Eight!"

Tucker stared at him in disbelief.

David also stared at him for several seconds, then said, "Give me a moment. I need to make a call." And he stood up and left the room.

"Agent Lewis has left the room at three-twenty-three p.m.," Tucker said for the record and then sat back, his arms folded, staring at Abbott.

"What's up, Doc?" Abbott asked.

"You're one sick son of a bitch," Tucker muttered. "You almost killed my partner. Would have if I hadn't stopped you."

"Them's the breaks, I guess," he replied, sounding totally at ease. "The silly bitch shoulda kept her nose out of what doesn't concern her. How is she, by the way?"

"She's fine," Tucker muttered.

"You are, aren't you?" he said. "You're screwin' her. I don't blame you. She's a looker, that's for sure."

It was at that moment that David reentered the room, just in time, as Tucker was about to go across the table at him.

"Whew, that was close. Did you know he was screwin' his partner?" Abbott said, grinning broadly. "So, what did your boss say?" he asked as David sat down. "Do I get a deal or not?"

"You get a deal," David said and nodded at the attorney. "Draw up the papers, and the director will sign them." He turned his attention back to Abbott and said, "So, start talking."

And he did. It turned out there were victims all over the tri-state area. Two in northern Alabama, two more in Georgia, and four in Tennessee, in Rhea, Marion, and Sequatchie counties, and one in Knoxville; thirteen in all. And all of them had stopped by the Pitt Stop, usually during visits to the various medical centers off Gunbarrel Road. That was the connection Tucker had been looking for, The Pitt Stop.

They questioned him at length for almost three more hours until David finally called it a day and Abbott was taken away.

Tucker and David left the police department together and stood for a moment in the parking lot.

David offered Tucker his hand, and Tucker shook it.

"You sure you won't take me up on my offer?" David asked.

Tucker shook his head, then said, "No, but thanks, David. As I told you, I'm done with all the BS and the bureaucracy."

David nodded. "We have a new president and a new AG. I have a feeling things are going to be different."

"How different can they be, David? The agency is a monolith. Nah, I'm done with it. Look, I have to go and see if Mallory's going home." He offered David his hand again and said, "I can't say it's been a pleasure, or fun, but I appreciate your help proving Mr. McNeer innocent."

David shook his hand and replied, "Stay safe, Tucker, and

look after that girl. She's a keeper. Call me if you change your mind." And with that, he turned and walked away to his car.

Tucker watched him go, then went to his car and called Mallory.

Mallory answered on the first ring. "Tucker. How did it go?"

"Well enough. I'll tell you all about it later. You ready to go home?"

"Yep, the doctor says I can. Jen wanted me to go and stay with her, but I told her no. You want to come and get me?"

"Of course. My place or yours?"

There was a moment of silence before she said, "Yours, but we'll have to pick up Annie."

Tucker smiled to himself, then said, "We can do that. I'll be there in thirty minutes."

"I'll be waiting," she said.

EPILOGUE

Peter Abbott was transferred to the FBI field office in Nashville two days later, on Saturday morning. It was over, all but the shouting, as they say. Over the next several weeks, he led them to the eight remaining bodies. At his trial, he pled guilty and was sentenced to life imprisonment on all charges.

Luthor McNeer was released from prison on New Year's Eve. Vinnie was there to meet him and to take him home. They hugged each other for the first time in more than eight years. It was a poignant moment.

Mallory spent the next seven days at Tucker's home recovering from her injuries. The head wound healed quickly, but the two broken ribs were painful and slow to heal. She'd been given Hydrocodone for the pain but refused to take it, preferring Tylenol instead.

She found the environment strange, at first. Tucker was the perfect gentleman, but their relationship had changed, and she could feel it stirring beneath the surface. So, it was three days later, on Sunday, when she decided to bring it to the surface.

"Tucker," she said as he poured them a second cup of coffee. "We've been dodging it for almost two weeks, but no more. We need to talk."

He looked at her, coffeepot in hand, not knowing what to say. "Oh yeah?"

She nodded. "Come and sit down."

He sat down and said, "Hey, we have a new case... and you'll never believe who it involves."

"Stop it," she whispered and reached out across the table and took his hand.

She looked into his eyes, her own eyes glistening, and said, "I'm in love with you, Tucker."

Thank you so much for reading, **Happily Never After**, the second book in the Randall & Carver Mysteries series. I hope you enjoyed it!

If you did, and you would like to know when the next book is coming out, or learn more about my books, please sign up for alerts and special deals on my website, Blair Howard Books. You can also Follow me on Amazon for new release announcements.

WHILE YOU WAIT FOR MY NEXT BOOK CHECK OUT MY OTHER BOOKS!

Have you read Jasmine?
Genesis?
How about Harry Starke?
Do you enjoy Spy Thrillers?

SIGN UP For Announcements & great deals!

PLUS you'll Unlock 20% Off

Get Exclusive Deals (As Part Of "The Family")

Visit www.BlairHowardBooks.com

If you don't see the pop up above, just click the blue unlock 20% off icon and enter your details.

Don't forget to confirm your email and whitelist (save as contact)BlairHoward@ blairhowardbooks.com to your email system.

Did you know you can buy signed paperbacks direct from my store?
Check them out! These are great gifts!

FROM BLAIR HOWARD

The Harry Starke Genesis Series
8 Books in Series as of 2024

The Harry Starke Series
24 Books in Series as of 2024

The Lt. Kate Gazzara Murder Files
20 Books in Series as of 2024

Randall And Carver Mysteries
2 Books in Series as of 2024

The Peacemaker Series
3 Books in Series as of 2024

The O'Sullivan Chronicles: Civil War Series
5 Books in Series as of 2024

FROM BLAIR C. HOWARD

The Sovereign Star Series
6 Books in Series as of 2024

ABOUT THE AUTHOR

Blair Howard is a retired journalist turned novelist. He's the author of more than 50 novels including the international best-selling Harry Starke series of detective crime stories, the Lt. Kate Gazzara Police Procedural series, the Harry Starke Genesis series, and the Randall & Carver Mysteries. He's also the author of the Peacemaker series of international spy thrillers and five Civil War/Western novels.

If you enjoy reading Science Fiction thrillers, Mr. Howard has made his debut into the genre with, The Sovereign Stars Series under the name, Blair C. Howard.

www.BlairHowardBooks.com

www.ingramcontent.com/pod-product-compliance
Lightning Source LLC
Chambersburg PA
CBHW011405010726
47495CB00009B/2786